"About the other day."

She waved him off.

"We're both working through some intense emotions," she said. "I think we know better than to go down that road again. Kissing was a mistake."

Confusion struck him. She'd changed gears on him so fast he hadn't had time to hit the clutch.

Because that kiss was the first thing that felt right to Wyatt in a long time. It was a dangerous sentiment considering he and Meg would have to figure out how to care for a child and stay on good terms.

Leading with his emotions would be a bullet through his chest when she pushed him away again. And she would.

For that little girl's sake he wouldn't allow that to happen. No matter how much he wanted to haul Meg against his chest and kiss her again.

KIDNAPPED AT CHRISTMAS

USA TODAY Bestselling Author

BARB HAN

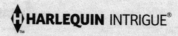

HARLEQUIN INTRIGUE®

Brandon, I'm amazed by your brilliance and kindness. I'm so very proud
of you. Jacob, I can't wait to play the games you're working so hard to
create. Tori, I love to watch you dance. From *Twinkle* to *Transformation*
to *It Is Done*, you have so many stories to tell.

Babe, my guy, for being my best friend and partner in crime. I love you.

To Michelle Spall for helping me see a new way to define home. I'm so
grateful for your friendship and am looking forward to many more
dance mom antics together.

ISBN-13: 978-1-335-63945-5

Kidnapped at Christmas

Copyright © 2018 by Barb Han

Recycling programs
for this product may
not exist in your area.

Printed in U.S.A.

HARLEQUIN®
www.Harlequin.com

USA TODAY bestselling author **Barb Han** lives in north Texas with her very own hero-worthy husband, three beautiful children, a spunky golden retriever/standard poodle mix and too many books in her to-read pile. In her downtime, she plays video games and spends much of her time on or around a basketball court. She loves interacting with readers and is grateful for their support. You can reach her at barbhan.com.

Books by Barb Han

Harlequin Intrigue

Crisis: Cattle Barge

Sudden Setup
Endangered Heiress
Texas Grit
Kidnapped at Christmas

Cattlemen Crime Club

Stockyard Snatching
Delivering Justice
One Tough Texan
Texas-Sized Trouble
Texas Witness
Texas Showdown

Mason Ridge

Texas Prey
Texas Takedown
Texas Hunt
Texan's Baby

The Campbells of Creek Bend

Witness Protection
Gut Instinct
Hard Target

Rancher Rescue

Harlequin Intrigue Noir

Atomic Beauty

Visit the Author Profile page at Harlequin.com.

CAST OF CHARACTERS

Meg Anderson—This single mother is ready to face the father of her newborn daughter and drop the bomb that he's a dad.

Wyatt Jackson—This Butler heir wants nothing to do with his relatives or their fortune after Mike Butler left Wyatt's mother barely able to care for him when he was an infant.

Aubrey Jackson—This two-month-old steals her father's heart from the minute he sets eyes on her, but her life is in danger, and it could be because of Wyatt's real last name—Butler.

Stephanie Gable—Meg's best friend is devastated when she's ambushed while caring for Aubrey.

Mary Jane Fjord—Meg's childhood best friend went missing years ago. Has the man who took her returned to claim Meg's daughter?

Jonathon Fjord—Losing his sister at such a young age left a mark.

Clayton Glass—The DNA on the missing girl's hair ribbon belongs to him, but who is he?

Sheriff Clarence Sawmill—This sheriff might be in over his head with a high-profile murder to solve and a town in chaos.

Maverick Mike Butler—Even in death this self-made Texas rancher has a few cards left to play.

Chapter One

"Why can't I think of one word to say to him?" Meg Anderson looked down at her sleeping angel, trying to psych herself up for the conversation that needed to take place with the baby's father.

"You're the best child advocate in Texas, Meg. The words will come." Meg's best friend and business partner, Stephanie Gable, walked over and ran her finger along two-month-old Aubrey's cheek.

"He deserves to know about her, right?" Meg already knew the answer, but she asked anyway. She'd do just about anything to gain a few more minutes of courage before walking out the door.

"He does." Stephanie's sympathetic tone struck a chord.

"I'm being totally unfair to her by keeping

her from her father." Tears burned the backs of Meg's eyes.

"That's right. If you can't do it for yourself, think of Aubrey." Stephanie seemed to be catching on. "It'll work out."

"What if he rejects her?" Meg tamped down the panic causing her heart to gallop.

"Then it's his loss." Stephanie didn't hesitate.

Meg made eyes at her friend. "You're absolutely right."

"What's the worst he can say?" Stephanie shot her what was supposed to be a nerve-fortifying look.

"I don't think I want to go there, not even in theory," Meg answered honestly. The rejection from her mother still stung even ten years after she'd walked out.

"You face bigger challenges every day and win." Stephanie was making good points, and yet Meg's courage still escaped her.

"Work challenges. This is personal." She twisted her fingers around the corner of the baby blanket swaddling her infant daughter, Aubrey. "And I'm pretty sure the statute of limitations and good taste has run out considering our daughter is two months old and I still haven't told him about her. How am I supposed to explain that?"

"If he's too stupid to figure out how you guys made a baby, he's definitely not worth all this stress." Stephanie laughed.

The joke was meant to ease the tension, so Meg smiled as she rolled the edge of the blanket in between her thumb and forefinger.

Normally the ploy would work. Not today. Not when Meg's thoughts were careening out of control.

"Okay, I can see my bad attempt at humor isn't helping. How about this? I'll take Aubrey to the park while you feel him out. See if he's ready." Stephanie's calm demeanor had little impact on Meg's frayed nerves. "You had good reasons for waiting. And he'd be crazy to turn his back on that little girl."

"A total nutcase," Meg agreed, gazing down at the sleeping bundle.

"She's perfect." Stephanie could hold her own with anyone in an argument. She was a huge asset to One Child—One Advocate. "She might just be the best baby in the world, bar none, and it would be his loss if he walked away from her." Stephanie smiled at Aubrey with the kind of sheer adoration reserved for aunts. She might not be a blood relative, but Stephanie was the closest thing to family Meg had aside from her daughter.

"The man should be given the option to be part of her life." Meg was steeling her resolve by picking up Aubrey. Holding her daughter, so much innocence, inspired her to do the right thing even when her nerves were frayed and her stomach threatened to revolt.

"I'll be right down the street with her at the park. You give me the green light and I'm there at the restaurant. If you don't pick up on the vibe that he wants to know or if he makes one wrong move before you tell him you can always do this another time."

"Will you text me first so I don't seem rude or obvious if I have to whip out my phone in front of him?" Meg hedged. Thinking through an exit strategy made her feel less trapped.

"Great idea. I'll take the baby for a lap or two before checking in." Stephanie picked up her purse. "The fresh air will be good for us both, and the park is so pretty this time of year. Plus, the mayor's lighting the Christmas tree at noon."

"She'd love that. It's probably just all these hormones and this time of year giving me jit-

ters." The first part was true enough. Meg
didn't want to acknowledge how much the
thought of seeing Wyatt Jackson again affected
her. This was the first time the Christmas sea-
son had brought a feeling of renewal and hope
instead of sadness and dread. The magic of the
holidays had always escaped Meg until having
Aubrey. Facing Wyatt with the news he was a
father stamped out all the newly gained warm-
and-fuzzy sentiment.

Stephanie shot a sympathetic look. "I know.
Everything in town's been strange ever since
Maverick Mike Butler's death this summer.
The whole town's been on edge. But everything's calming down and slowly returning to
normal. It's only a matter of time before the
sheriff finds the person responsible and we can
put all this behind us. You have a new baby
and lots of memories to look forward to. And
it's nice to focus on something besides murder
for a change."

Meg nodded. The town had been through
a lot since its wealthiest and most infamous
resident was killed on his ranch this past summer. But it was more than that. The holidays
brought back a memory of being interviewed
for hours. The unspoken accusations had been

so obvious that even a ten-year-old girl had understood them. Meg shivered involuntarily, thinking about the past. She couldn't bring herself to talk about it with anyone. She needed to focus on something else. Bad thoughts had a way of multiplying, causing her to tumble down a slippery slope of pain and regret.

Meg turned her attention to her sleeping baby. The change in Meg this year was because of Aubrey. That little girl brightened everything she touched. Her baby held a special kind of magic that made Meg want to believe in miracles again, precisely the innocent sentiment that would end up crushing her in—she checked her watch—less than five minutes.

She shouldered the diaper bag. "Ready?"

When Meg had become too sick to drive herself to a doctor visit, Stephanie had stepped up to help. Not long after, her work partner had found herself in a bind when her two-year relationship ended and she had no place to live. Meg had volunteered to room together and the friendship had blossomed from there. It was nice to have that in her life after keeping herself isolated for so long.

Stephanie examined Meg with a questioning look. "I am."

"It's just a conversation," Meg said to herself as she walked outside, bracing herself against the blast of frigid air. Her small SUV was parked in the lot behind the office. "I speak to people every day."

"And you're pretty darn good at it, too." Stephanie closed and locked the door behind them. It was Friday and they'd let the receptionist go early so she could watch the tree-lighting ceremony. "But anything about this guy gives you pause and I'm only two blocks away. I can be at the restaurant in less than five minutes." Stephanie snapped her fingers.

Meg froze as an awkward thought struck. "What if he doesn't remember me?"

"It's only been a year, Meg. You said that he'd been clear about not being the type to settle down, but I seriously doubt you'd spend time with anyone who was that much of a jerk." Stephanie jangled her keys. "Besides, I'm following you in my car in case you both remember all too well and decide to get to know each other again while I babysit." Stephanie wiggled her eyebrows.

Meg held back the laugh trying to force its way out of her throat. Wyatt Jackson didn't want anything to do with her.

"I had to email him half a dozen times in order to get a response. If he remembers me at all from a year ago, he obviously wasn't too impressed." Meg secured Aubrey in her car seat in Stephanie's car. The baby stretched but didn't wake. She'd had a bottle twenty minutes ago so, fingers crossed, that should buy Meg a couple of hours to do what she should've done months ago before the baby arrived. Shoving the guilt aside, she climbed into the driver's seat.

Meg glanced around with that awful feeling of someone watching her. Her stress levels were already on an upward trajectory and this made it worse. It was probably nothing more than the thought of facing her baby's father that had her insides braided and the tiny hairs on her arms standing at attention. Or maybe it was the time of year. The holidays. The cold. The memories...

Meg glanced at the rearview. No one was there. She started the vehicle.

Wyatt Jackson was just a man like any other. This wasn't the time for her brain to point out that he was intelligent, successful and unnervingly gorgeous. In retrospect, the man seemed almost superhuman to her. But then, he'd given her the absolute best gift in her life, her daughter, and that was likely the reason she'd built him up so much in her mind.

Meg checked the rearview one more time, making sure that Stephanie had cleared the parking spot behind her. She glanced at the backup camera as she pressed the gas pedal. Something crossed the corner of the screen.

Heart jackhammering, she touched the brake.

What was back there? An animal?

A tiny little thing darted toward the trees, yellow stripes streaking past the driver's side. It was just a cat, barely more than a kitten.

Hands shaking, Meg white-knuckled the steering wheel, trying to calm her rattled nerves by sheer force of will.

There was nothing to be afraid of.

Right?

CHRISTMAS MIGHT ONLY be weeks away, but the holidays were something Wyatt Jackson would have no trouble skipping over altogether. New Year's was more his style with its all-night partying and the attitude of ringing in the New Year with free-flowing booze and a carefree attitude.

Speaking of which, receiving an email from the blond-haired beauty Wyatt had spent time with last year had caught him off guard. She'd made it look easy to ignore his repeated phone calls this time last year, so he'd returned the favor by deleting her messages when she'd first contacted him.

In fact, in the past twelve months he'd done his level best to forget she existed. Although part of him had known that would be impossible given that he couldn't seem to shake the feel of her soft skin on his fingertips, her intellect or the easy way she made him laugh.

The last email from Meg had seemed urgent, and to make matters even more interesting Maverick Mike Butler's lawyer had been hot on Wyatt's tail to get him to come to Cattle Barge. Mike Butler had been one of Texas's most colorful citizens. A billionaire cattle rancher who'd been murdered on his own property this summer had sent the media into a feeding frenzy.

Ed Staples, the family's lawyer, had seemed downright shocked that Wyatt already knew he was Mike Butler's illegitimate son. Probably because Wyatt hadn't made a single attempt to contact the estate—and thereby claim his right to the Butler fortune. Wyatt had made a success of himself on his own terms and had no need for a handout from the family who'd left his mother pregnant and destitute.

The first thing Wyatt had noticed when he hit Cattle Barge city limits was the swarm of media people. The town was still overrun months after Butler's murder, although reporters were starting to write fluff. News about the famous will being read on Christmas Eve splashed across headlines on every outlet. Maverick Mike could take his money and shove it up his...

Wyatt realized he'd white-knuckled the steering wheel and laughed at himself. The holidays had soured his mood, and he had no plans to let emotions get in the way of what he hoped would be a hot reunion between him and the blonde. Besides, he couldn't imagine that Maverick Mike's legitimate kids would welcome him with open arms. Making the Butler heirs uncomfortable wasn't the main reason Wyatt had hit the highway leading to Cattle Barge. He saw it more as a fringe benefit.

Wyatt knew the reason he'd been summoned, and to say he had mixed feelings about Maverick Mike Butler being his father was a lot like saying ghost peppers burned the tongue. Was he a Butler? His mother had said so, but in his heart he could never be connected to the man who'd walked away from her, from *him*.

Wyatt didn't want the man's money. His twenty-fifth Tiko Taco restaurant was about to open and he didn't need a handout from anyone. Wyatt had learned how to work hard for his successes and he enjoyed the fruits of his labor to the fullest.

The Butlers weren't the real reason he'd accepted the invitation to meet the family. There was another benefit to coming to Cattle Barge— seeing Meg Anderson again. He'd needed a good reason to show, convincing himself that a reunion wasn't pull enough and especially with the way she'd left things. To prove a point to himself—the point being that he didn't need her—he'd taken his time to return her emails.

That her tone had intensified, saying that they needed to meet got his curiosity going. They'd spent time together and—according to his memory—had one helluva good time before she'd ditched him. She'd cut off communication a few months after their smoking-hot affair started, leaving him scratching his head at what he'd done wrong.

Granted, he wasn't the relationship type by a long shot and he'd been up-front about it with her. He was always honest. And he knew deep down that one of them was bound to walk away first sooner or later. Normally he hit the door, not the other way around, and that was most likely the reason she was still on his mind a year later. He could make that concession.

He'd been clear about his intentions, and although he'd enjoyed her company—he could further admit that *enjoyed* put it lightly—they hadn't been together long enough for real heartbreak. And yet there'd been an uncomfortable feeling in his chest that felt a lot like a hole ever since she'd walked away.

Wyatt flipped the radio channel to his favorite country-and-western station. The breakup song playing reminded him of how he'd felt when Meg cut off communication. Now he was a bad cliché, and that just worsened his mood.

And even though Christmas was coming, he was most definitely not a ho-ho-ho type. Kris Kringle had never been more than a fat man in a silly suit. Wyatt tried to convince himself one more time that he didn't care what Meg had to tell him. He was doing her a favor by showing up to hear her out and he needed to be in town anyway, so he might as well see what she wanted.

He parked at the Home Grown Foods Restaurant and ignored the fact that his pulse kick-started with each forward step toward the door. What was he—a teenager again? That ship had sailed long ago, and Wyatt didn't appreciate the blast from the past making his collar feel stifling and his palms warm and sweaty.

The restaurant, located in the center of Main Street, had all of seven patrons. Traffic alone should've dictated a full house, although he remembered spotting a sign on his way in with details about a tree lighting at the park. He'd only been half paying attention.

Meg was hard to miss in her spot at the four-top table dead center in the room, and it was more than just her beauty that drew him toward her, although she looked even better than he remembered. She gave him one of those awkward morning-after smiles, the nervous kind with thin lips and scarcely any teeth showing. Even so, she was stunning and his heart reacted to seeing her by ratcheting up a few notches.

Acknowledging her with a nod, he removed his Stetson and closed the distance between them.

"Thanks for coming." She motioned toward

the chair and quickly pulled her hand back like an alligator might bite it. "Please, take a seat."

The muscles on her forehead were pinched, which did nothing to dull her beauty as she sat on the edge of her seat. All hope this was going to be fun-filled day of reunion sex after a quick greeting and a decent meal died.

"You said this was important." He took the chair opposite her, reminding himself not to get too comfortable. He leaned back, crossed his legs and touched his fingertips together, forming a steeple. The most beautiful pair of sky-blue eyes framed by thick dark eyelashes stared back at him. Her eyes were the color of summer.

"It is." Blond locks spilled down her back. Was she this stunning before? Damn. She was and more.

Seeing her again awakened cells he thought were beyond resuscitation. Too bad she wanted something from him. And then he thought about it. News must be out that he was a Butler. A small town like Cattle Barge would have trouble keeping anything secret for long. Was she making a play for his inheritance? His heart argued against the idea even as the thought made him frown. Besides, he had no plans to claim anything about being a Butler, so she'd be out of luck.

A waitress brought over a menu. She was short, maybe five-feet-three inches, and had mousy brown hair. Her name tag read Hailey. The woman was the complete opposite of Meg, who had those long legs and shiny blond locks.

"Can I get you anything to drink?" Hailey asked.

"No. Thank you, Hailey." He didn't figure this conversation was going to take long enough to stick around. Meg would make her demand. He'd say no. Problem solved.

Ignoring the tug at his heart, he said, "I'm not staying."

Meg let out a little grunt.

"You sure about that?" Hailey asked with a smile and a wink.

"Never been more certain of anything in my life." Out of respect for his companion, he didn't flirt back.

"Let me know if you change your mind," Hailey said with a pout.

There was another emotion radiating off Meg—impatience. Or it could be jealousy, but that was most likely wishful thinking on his part. Sue him. She was even more beautiful than he remembered, and another pang of something—remorse?—hit as he acknowledged to himself she didn't seem to want to be there any more than he did. At least he was trying to make the best out of a bad situation. What was her excuse?

Her arms were crossed and her gaze laser focused.

"Might as well go ahead and spit it out." He didn't bother hiding his impatience. "What do you want from me?"

A sound ripped from her throat and she made a move toward her purse.

"Do us both a favor." She looked him square in the eyes. "Forget I called."

"Suit yourself," he said without conviction as he stood.

Wyatt turned around and walked right out the door.

Chapter Two

With every step the handsome cowboy took toward the parking lot, Meg's pulse climbed another notch. Let him leave and it was all over. She couldn't imagine finding the courage to contact him again, and even if she did he wouldn't take her calls.

Seeing him again, all bronzed hair and steel-gray eyes with thick lashes, had thrown her off. The restaurant should've been full over the lunch hour but she'd forgotten about the midday tree-lighting ceremony in the park. The place must be bustling about now, and she figured that was half the reason she hadn't heard from Stephanie yet.

Meg pushed off the chair and followed Wyatt. A young guy held the door open for her, but their feet collided and she had to take a couple of steps to recover her balance.

She acknowledged his mumbled apology with a nod. Her gaze was locked onto Wyatt's back side as she ignored the sensual shivers running through her.

The fact that he'd been clear about flying solo had been the exact reason she'd ended their fling last year and walked away before her emotions got involved.

"Wait," she said to his back, a strong one at that. Birds fluttered in her chest. When he didn't stop, she added, "Please."

Wyatt slowed his pace, which allowed her to catch up to his long strides without breaking into a run.

"I'm sorry about before…" Now at his side, she could see him smirking. Meg stopped. "I have something serious to say, but if this is just a game to you then forget it."

Wyatt turned to face her and put all signs of his playboy swagger in check.

Wow. Meg had been nervous before, but she had totally underestimated how much harder this was going to be in person while staring into his eyes. Her legs threatened to give.

"Last year, I stopped returning your calls—"

He brought his hand up to stop her.

"If that's why you called me here, save it.

It was a long time ago and I don't need an explanation. We had fun. You moved on. End of story." Was there a momentary flicker of… *hurt?*…in his eyes? Meg must be crazy and seeing imaginary things. What was next? Unicorns? She'd been reading too many fairy tales to her daughter because her mind was flirting with believing them.

He made a move to walk away again, and the pressure mounted…

"We had more than fun. We had a baby," she blurted out, her pulse pounding wildly in part because of what she'd just shared and in part because of the strong virile male standing two feet in front of her.

He looked her up and down like he was evaluating her for a trip to the psych ward. His eyes grazed a hot trail as they lingered on the curve of her hips and then the fullness of her breasts. An unwelcome sensation of warmth slid along her belly and heated her inner thighs despite the frigid December temperatures.

"How do you know it's mine?" That question was the equivalent of a bucket of ice water dumped over her head.

"You were the only possibility." She brought

her fisted hand to rest on her hip and her body shivered to stave off the cold.

Wyatt glanced around. "I don't exactly see a baby, so…"

"She's at the park." Meg fumbled inside her purse for her cell, willing her shaky hands to calm down. After his accusation, they were trembling with anger. She needed to check her texts to see if Stephanie had tried to reach her. "She's eight weeks old and I haven't slept since she was born, so excuse me if I'm a little rattled." She threw one of her hands up in the air.

"If you're after the Butler fortune you're going about it the wrong way." The words knifed her chest. She'd expected him to be surprised but not condemn her as money-grubbing crackpot, but hold on a minute. Had she heard him right?

"What does my daughter have to do with the Butlers? Your last name is Jackson." Now it was Meg's turn to look at him like he'd lost his mind. Although, she shouldn't be surprised at the news. Maverick Mike Butler had fathered at least one other child that no one knew about.

Wyatt stared at her, same as before, with a raised brow and unbelievable expression.

"No, I'm not in need of psychiatric care." She

located her cell and white-knuckled it. "And I do have a baby."

Meg entered her screensaver password and noticed there was still no text from Stephanie. An uneasy feeling gripped her as she stuck her phone out at Wyatt. A picture of Aubrey was her wallpaper and, therefore, proof. "See."

He nodded as he scrutinized the image.

"You still haven't answered my question. What does Aubrey have to do with the Butlers?" Her patience was running thin and she really was starting to get worried about Stephanie.

Wyatt looked at a loss for words.

"Never mind. Excuse me for a second while I make a call. My friend took my—" she flashed eyes at him "—*our* daughter for a walk around the park. She was supposed to text me in case things went sour…" Meg ran her finger along Stephanie's name. She didn't dare turn her back on Wyatt for fear he'd disappear even though she wanted to make this call in private. The cell ran straight into voice mail and her pulse shot up a couple more notches. "Stephanie, give me a call as soon as you get this. Hope everything is okay."

Wyatt, who had been quiet until now, said, "I'm sure everything's all right."

"It's not like her not to do something if she says she's going to." Meg started to pace, torn between walking away from him—and possibly never seeing him again—and checking on her daughter.

"Do you trust your friend?" he asked.

"Absolutely."

"Then you have to believe that she wouldn't do anything to put your daughter in harm's way. That's really what you're worried about, right? Something bad happening to..." He seemed to be searching for the name so she supplied it.

"Aubrey."

His jaw muscle ticked. "Right. You said something about a tree-lighting ceremony and that's probably what the traffic I drove in to get here was for. Thus, the reason I was late. They could be playing holiday music. She most likely can't hear her cell."

"Wouldn't we hear if it was *that* loud?" she asked.

"It's two blocks away from the restaurant. I doubt it." He was making sense, being rational, while her over-the-top protective instinct was waging war on her insides. The two had driven separate vehicles because Stephanie had errands to run later.

"I have a bad feeling." She couldn't shake it no matter how hard she tried.

"You and every mother I've ever known." Wyatt's steel gaze intensified.

She looked at him, shocked.

"What?" He lifted a shoulder.

"How many like me have there been?" Astonishment flushed her cheeks.

"Like you?" He shot a look. "None."

"Then how do you… Oh, right, you had a mother." She didn't figure him the type to notice the little things. "Everyone does. Even someone like—"

"You really don't like me very much, do you?" he said with half a smirk and that infuriating twinkle in his eye that had been so good at seducing her.

"I'm sorry. It's just ever since my—" she glanced up at him "—*our* daughter was born I've been on high alert, afraid something could happen to her. She's so tiny and fragile except when she cries. Then I know there's a tiger in there waiting to come out. But the rest of the time she's just this little thing who's totally dependent on me and I'm trying my best not to mess everything up." Had all that really just come out? Wow. Meg was on the verge of a meltdown. She was normally more of the quiet type.

Wyatt seemed too stunned to speak.

"None of which is your problem." She glanced at the time. More than half an hour had passed and still no word from Stephanie.

"We can head down there to the park, to see for ourselves." He was extending an olive branch and she would take it.

"Thank you. I'd like that a lot actually." Meg started toward the park, remembering that although he might have the swagger of a playboy and was all alpha male, she'd been drawn to his kindness in the first place. There wasn't anything sexier than a strong man who wasn't afraid to show he had a beating heart in his chest.

"I'm not claiming responsibility for her," he clarified, and it was so cold outside she could see his breath. So much for the warmth.

WYATT STARED AT the woman who was walking so fast he had to hustle to keep pace. His judgment with people and especially women was normally spot-on, and he hadn't pegged Meg Anderson as unstable or a gold digger.

In fact, she'd seemed like the most grounded, intelligent woman he'd been with in a long time, possibly ever. Her sharp mind was what he'd missed most about her. Since their tryst he'd compared every date to her and no one seemed to measure up. Even sex had been lacking, but that was a whole other story that made him think he might be losing his edge. So, he was even more shocked by her whipping out the baby card. Was there even a child? *His child?* This whole conversation left him scratching his head and an unsettled feeling gnawed at his gut.

He took off his coat and placed it around her arms, realizing she didn't have any covering on her shoulders. She must've left her jacket on the chair back where he'd last seen it.

He didn't have the heart to walk away while she was so distraught. Even though she'd shown him the pic of the cute infant on her phone, he couldn't ignore the possibility that she'd jumped off the deep end. Maybe she'd been on mood-regulating drugs when they'd spent time together. Maybe she'd stopped taking them and this was the real her.

His logical mind wrestled against the possibility, but that could just be his pride unable to accept that he'd made such a wide turn with his judgment before. Wyatt had always considered himself more intelligent than that. As they said, the proof was in the pudding and this "pudding" was starting to unravel in front of his eyes.

When he really looked at her, he couldn't ignore the changes in her body. Her hips had more pronounced curves, which were even sexier now. There were definite changes in her breasts. They'd been full before but not quite this generous.

Even tired, she was still one of the most beautiful women he'd ever seen. He told himself the only reason he was noticing any of the changes in her was because he was trying to determine if she needed to be driven to Kruger Belton Mental facility for evaluation and not because he cared or was still attracted to her. His heart had fisted a little bit when he'd first seen her. He did care, generally speaking.

The park was crowded. Holiday music filled the air. Families walked in clumps, smiling and singing along with Christmas carols. It was something out of a Norman Rockwell painting and definitely not Wyatt's scene.

"They aren't here." Meg stopped and looked at him, clearly flustered. She had that panicked-mother look even though he wouldn't know from personal experience. His had been too exhausted working to keep food on the table to get too emotional. He'd known his mother loved him and the fact he'd grown up in poverty was all the more reason to be proud of the success-ful taco franchise he'd built from a food truck.

Meg dug in her purse and pulled out a baby's cloth with little owls on it.

"Was she supposed to bring the baby to the restaurant?" He had no idea of the protocol in dealing with a nearly hysterical woman, but he could see from the way she twisted the baby's cloth in her hands that she was working herself up. Experience with women had taught him that this was not the time to tell her to *calm down*.

"Stephanie was supposed to text first." Meg worked the cloth in her hands.

"Her battery could've died." She winced at that last word.

"I guess." That cloth in her hands was about to become pulp.

Wyatt reached out to touch her shoulder in an attempt to reassure her but was left with a sizzle on his fingertips. He almost pulled his hand back but decided to ignore the frissons of heat.

Hot or not, this one was off-limits, and especially with the bomb she'd dropped on him earlier.

Still, he couldn't help but feel sorry for her. The child, real or imagined, was obviously very important to her. So much so that she was trembling.

And then she looked up at him with those blue eyes that he'd liked looking into right before he fell off the cliff during sex. *Okay, not the time for that thought, Jackson.*

"I can't imagine how all this must look from your point of view. Thank you for the coat. I must've left mine in the restaurant. I was in such a hurry to catch you because I knew if you left it was over. I'd never have the courage to email again. You should know that I don't want anything from you. I just thought you had a right to know about your daughter."

Whether he believed her or not didn't matter. She seemed vulnerable, and that pierced his armor. "We'll figure this out."

Her phone buzzed and her ringtone sounded, same ones as before. He should know. He'd been the one to program the song into her new phone when she couldn't figure out how to change the basic sound.

A look of sheer relief flooded her tense expression as she checked the screen. "It's Stephanie."

Wyatt needed to clear his head so he could face the Butler family this afternoon. To say this day was throwing curveball after curveball was a lot like saying Texas highways were crowded. At least Meg had received the call she'd been waiting for and that was a relief.

His respite was short-lived as Meg dropped to her knees.

"Tell me where you are and I'll be there in two seconds." Her voice shook and panic radiated from her.

He offered a hand up, which she took. The color had drained from her face as she glanced around. "The Butler Fountain?" She paused. "I know exactly where that is."

Whatever her friend was saying wasn't good, and he figured this day was about to get even longer.

"Did you give the sheriff your statement?" She paused again. "Do it right now. Tell them everything you just told me. I'm almost there."

Now his curiosity was getting the best of him as Meg broke into a run.

He followed, easily keeping pace even though Meg was still obviously in shape. She gripped her cell as she raced toward the planned site of the Mike Butler Memorial Fountain.

A small crowd had gathered, facing away from the tree. There was a woman on the ground, her legs curled up and her face scrunched in pain and panic.

"What's going on?" he asked Meg as they neared the woman.

"I'm so sorry. I don't know what happened," the woman he presumed to be Stephanie said through sobs. "I was walking along fine and then I blacked out." Her hand came up to the back of her head to rub. "Ouch…" She blinked in panic, tears welling. "I came to and she was gone. Someone took her. Someone kidnapped Aubrey. They must've taken everything, the stroller and the diaper bag. All I remember is blacking out."

The most heartbreaking sound tore from Meg's throat.

Wyatt's head nearly exploded and an ache ripped through his chest. He couldn't figure out why he'd have such a strong reaction to a child's kidnapping when, first, he'd never even met the little tyke and, second, he still wasn't convinced she belonged to him.

His heart didn't seem to need confirmation one way or the other.

Chapter Three

"Did you call the sheriff?" Meg asked, looking like her world had just tipped on its axis in the same way Wyatt's just had. But there was no way he could care this much about a child he'd never met. He chalked his feelings up to sympathy for the mother and the heartbreaking situation.

"I did." A woman stepped forward. She was young, mid-twenties, and clutching a small child's hand. The little boy couldn't be more than three or four years old. "I wish I'd seen more. I heard someone scream and ran over to see what happened. I was too late."

Meg thanked her.

"He's on his way." Stephanie glanced around at the gathering crowd, looking bewildered. "There was a guy—he was wearing one of those forest green park-maintenance uniforms—and he said he saw everything before taking off in that direction." She pointed east. "Said he'd be right back."

Meg looked on the verge of crumpling. The more people who gathered around the less likely it would be for him or Meg to see someone escaping with the stroller. Wyatt glanced at Meg.

"What color stroller am I looking for?" he asked.

"Red with big wheels to take it jogging." She glanced from him to Stephanie with the most sorrowful look on her face.

Wyatt glanced around at the small crowd. "Did any of you see anything unusual or anyone hurrying out of this area with a red stroller?" The odds were slim anyone would notice details like that, but it was worth asking.

Heads shook.

"There was a lot going on and the music was too loud. I was afraid to wake her, so I stayed back here by the benches. I was worried that Meg would text and I would miss it." Stephanie sobbed.

"You did the right thing." Wyatt had no idea what to say, but he wished he could make the situation okay for both of them. Stephanie seemed like a nice person and he already knew Meg was. At least she hadn't been lying about there being a child. Obviously, there was. No one would go through this much trouble to set up a lie.

"Go. Look for her. I'm fine," Stephanie said, trying to push to her feet. She wobbled and a Good Samaritan steadied her by grabbing her arm in time before she landed on her bottom. She thanked him.

"We'll stay with her," the woman with the child said.

"Did you see anything?" Wyatt asked Stephanie.

"No. I was walking with the stroller before I felt something hard hit the back of my head and then I blacked out. Next thing I knew the park worker was beside me asking if I was okay and I had a blinding headache." She touched a spot behind her left ear.

Meg hopped onto a nearby bench and scanned the area.

"See anything up there?" Wyatt asked. He tried to convince himself that he'd feel this panicked whether the child might be his or not. An infant had been kidnapped, and he could admit that he still had residual feelings for the baby's mother. The little girl didn't have to belong to him for his heart to go out to Meg. If he could help her find her baby he would. And if she kept on insisting the baby was his, he'd ask for a DNA test before he got too worked up. Keeping a level head in challenging times had earned Wyatt his solid reputation in the business world and helped him expand to twenty-five locations. This was no different.

He joined Meg on the park bench. There were too many people spreading in all different directions. The ceremony had ended, which was the perfect time to execute this kind of crime because there was chaos while families exited the park area and spilled into the parking lot.

There was no way he was going to find the person responsible at this rate. He couldn't justify standing around and watching all this heartbreak, either.

"Text me and let me know what the sheriff says. I have to do something," Meg shouted to her friend, and he completely understood the sentiment. He was having the same conversation in his head.

Meg was on the verge of tears as she turned to look at him. "I don't see any sign of her."

"If I was going to commit the crime, I'd park in the closest spot." He pointed to the nearest parking lot, which was slowly emptying. There was a line to exit, and the park's location in the center of town off the main square caused traffic to move slowly. "Maybe we can spot your daughter in a car on the way out of the lot."

"It's worth a try." Meg sounded hopeless as he held out his hand. She took it. A simple gesture really, but when their hands made contact a fire bolt shot straight up his arm. He ignored it as best he could and took off running. With their hands linked, Meg kept pace and he was pretty sure it was from pure adrenaline.

"Maybe there," she said through gulps of air as they darted toward the light that regulated the exit. "I see the handle of a stroller in the back window and it's red."

Wyatt let her hand loose so he could push forward and catch the white minivan before the light turned and the vehicle disappeared. From this angle, he couldn't get a good look at the plate. He pushed his legs harder, leaving Meg several strides behind. If he could get to the minivan in time maybe he could put this whole ordeal to rest.

The minivan was close, but the light could

turn at any second. Wyatt pushed harder until his thighs burned and his lungs threatened to burst. He could see there was only a driver and the figure was large enough to be male.

"Hold on," he shouted to the van's driver. The window was up and the man didn't so much as flinch.

As the light changed, Wyatt closed in on the van. He was so close. Dammit. There were three cars ahead of the minivan, not close enough for Wyatt to catch. The cars moved and the minivan turned left, which was the opposite side of Wyatt. What an unlucky break.

Wyatt shot in between two cars. One of the drivers laid on his horn and shouted a few terse words. Wyatt had no idea where Meg was and he didn't risk turning back to look. The minivan was going at least thirty-five miles an hour. If he could catch a break and the light at the corner turned to red… Scratch that. Wyatt had never been lucky and that's how he'd learned to work hard for everything he'd built.

Brake lights renewed his hope as he turned on the speed he'd known as a runner in high school. Although that had been a long time ago, he worked out and kept in shape.

The van disappeared around the corner before the light changed.

"Wyatt." Meg's voice rippled through him. There was a mix of hope and relief in the sound of her tone. "I got her."

He immediately turned tail and saw a man in a forest green uniform standing next to Meg, who was holding a baby. He made a beeline toward the trio, driven by something deep inside. Was it a primal need to see if her child belonged to him? Would he even be able to tell by looking at her one time?

Meg stood there, baby pressed to her chest and her face awash with relief. She was gently rocking the crying infant. An odd thought hit: No one had better get close to her or the baby. He was struck with something else that felt a lot like longing, but Wyatt didn't go there. He'd missed Meg. He could own up to it. That's as far as his feelings went, he reminded himself.

"I'm Wyatt Jackson." He stuck out his hand to the park worker. "And I can't thank you enough for what you did."

The man bent forward, panting as he took the outstretched hand. "Name's Cecil. And I'm just—" he paused to take a breath "—glad I was there to help." Cecil grabbed at his right side. "He got away, ditched the stroller by pushing it toward traffic. I had to make a choice to save her or catch him." He paused long enough to take in another breath. "His back was to me the whole time. I couldn't get a good look at his face."

"You did the right thing, Cecil." Relief washed over Wyatt. This morning had been right up there with… He didn't want to think about the other depressing event that came with the holidays.

The baby was in her mother's arms, safe. Crisis averted. That was all he would allow himself to focus on.

"Are you okay to walk?" he asked Cecil.

The man nodded.

The crime scene had been cordoned off, and a deputy was asking people to go back to work or home. Stephanie flew toward Meg and the baby; tears streamed down both women's faces.

A man by the name of Clarence Sawmill introduced himself as the sheriff. Cecil recounted his story to Sawmill, who shook his head as he recorded details. His lips formed a grim line. Middle-aged, his eyes had the white outline of sunglasses on otherwise tanned skin. Deep grooves in his forehead and hard brackets around his mouth outlined the man's stress levels. He was on high alert and, from the looks of him, had been since news broke of Maverick Mike's death five months ago.

"Our family-oriented town doesn't usually see much of a spike in crime." Sawmill shook his head. For a split second his gaze stopped on Wyatt and he seemed to be sizing him up. The sheriff looked like he hadn't slept in as many months and he probably hadn't, considering Mike Butler's murder still hadn't been solved. Sawmill seemed like the kind of guy who would take his citizens' welfare to heart.

The sheriff was holding an evidence bag.

"What did you find?" Wyatt asked.

"A child's hair ribbon. It's probably not connected. More than likely came out of a little girl's hair while she was attending the tree lighting." Sawmill pinched the bridge of his nose like he was trying to stem a raging headache. "My deputies will process the scene and we'll keep you posted if anything relevant turns up."

Meg thanked the sheriff as she gently bounced the baby, who had settled down in her mother's comforting arms. He had to admit Meg seemed content with the job of mother.

The sheriff asked Meg a few routine-sounding questions. Her body language tensed when she spoke to Sawmill, but Wyatt figured it was justifiable under the circumstances. She was being asked if there was a reason anyone she knew would try to kidnap her infant child.

"We have a potential witness already on his way to the station to work with a sketch artist while the details are still fresh," Sawmill said. "We'll want you to come in and take a look as soon as we have an image in case you can identify him."

Given the person had tried to take the baby while she was with Stephanie, Wyatt doubted that was likely.

Even so, he planned to reschedule his meeting with the Butler family lawyer. This day had taken unexpected turn after unexpected turn and, after getting a good look at Meg's daughter, he had a feeling the day wasn't done with him yet.

DINNER WAS HOURS away and yet all Meg wished for was a hot bath, a warm bed and sleep. Wyatt had said he'd been called away to a meeting, but Meg figured he needed air after the day's events. Meg and Stephanie returned to the office since it was closer to the sheriff's office and Aubrey had a pack-and-play crib there.

Stephanie had insisted on sticking around even though Meg had begged her friend to go to the ER instead. The most she would agree to was allowing an EMT to check her out at the scene.

"How's your head?" Meg asked her friend.

"It's been worse," Stephanie said with a crooked smile.

"I still think we should swing by the hospital," Meg said.

"My name is Stephanie Gable. It's three weeks until Christmas. I live at 1212 Farm Road 236. With you, who should learn to relax a little more and stop washing every dish before it hits the sink, by the way." She made eyes at Meg. "How's that?"

"I think you took a bigger hit than we first thought," she quipped, and they both smiled. Meg's died on her lips the minute her cell rang.

A glance at the screen said it was the sheriff's office. She took the call.

"We have an image to work with but, to be honest, it isn't much to go on," he said. Any hope this case could be sewn up and a criminal taken off the streets soon died.

"I'll let Wyatt know and we'll be there as soon as we can," she informed him before ending the call and texting Wyatt.

An immediate response came: Stay where you are and I'll pick you up.

"What did the sheriff say?" Stephanie was studying Meg's reaction.

"He didn't sound encouraged," Meg admitted.

"We'll figure this out." Her friend's words were meant to reassure, but did nothing to ease the knot braiding her stomach.

Meg glanced down at her sleeping baby. She'd been unable to move from the little girl's side since... Meg couldn't even think about what had happened, what *could* have happened, without tears springing to her eyes. She was so grateful to have her daughter back where she belonged.

What kind of person tried to take a baby from her mother three weeks before Christmas? Granted, the person had tried to take the little girl from Stephanie, but the attacker didn't know the difference.

Skipping lunch had been a bad idea even though Meg doubted she could get or keep anything down. A headache was trying to form in the spot right between her eyes.

Within fifteen minutes, Aubrey had been fed and the diaper bag packed.

"He's on his way?" Stephanie paced in the kitchenette of their office.

"He should be here any minute." Meg cradled the warm, sleeping baby in her arms. Her miracle, considering she'd never expected to have a traditional life of marriage and a family. "You should sit down."

Stephanie shot her an apprehensive look.

"Well, then maybe you should rethink going to the hospital to get checked out." Meg eyed the cup of coffee in Stephanie's shaking hand, wishing her friend had gone for the calming tea, instead.

"The ibuprofen is already kicking in. I'll be fine. I'm just so glad…" Another stream of tears slid down Stephanie's cheeks. She turned her back and sniffed.

"Let's not even go there. None of this is your fault." Meg held her baby a little closer. "And she's right here. Fine. Look at her."

A knock on the glass out front startled them both.

"That's probably him," Meg said.

"Stay right here. I'll check." Stephanie was out of the room in a flash and Meg figured her friend needed to work off some of her stress energy. The adrenaline would wear off soon, and she was afraid Stephanie was in for one monster headache when it did.

Her own nerves were on edge after the day's events and thinking about seeing Wyatt again didn't help. Based on his actions earlier, he planned to be in Aubrey's life, and Meg would have to get used to her body's reaction to him. Her heart seized a little bit at the thought he didn't want to be in hers, too. What did she expect?

Sure, they'd connected last year with chemistry she'd never experienced before, and that spark between them, mentally and physically, had produced amazingly hot sex. *And a baby*, a little voice reminded, grounding her.

"Ready?" Wyatt examined her and the baby in her arms. He was the kind of man who would do the right thing by his child no matter how he felt personally about the child's mother. On the one hand, there was something encouraging about the sentiment. At least Aubrey would have a father.

Meg stood and reached for the diaper bag.

Wyatt moved beside her in a beat, taking it from her. He hadn't asked to hold the baby yet, and this was the closest he'd been to her since they'd found her. Not exactly encouraging, but it could've been so much worse.

Based on the crease in his forehead, the one he got when he was deeply contemplating something, he needed a little time to process. His daughter had almost been kidnapped.

"Wyatt, meet your daughter, Aubrey," Meg said.

A flash of emotion passed behind his eyes as he looked at her but he seemed to get hold of it. "She's a pretty little girl."

"Do you want to hold her?" she asked.

"Not yet," he said.

Fifteen minutes later, the four of them arrived at the sheriff's office.

Janis, the sheriff's receptionist, rose to her feet. "We've spoken on the phone a few times. Come on in. The sheriff is waiting for you." She wrapped Meg and the baby in a big hug before leading them down the hall.

Sawmill got to his feet and extended his hand. "Please, sit down."

The sheriff's office was large, simple. There was a huge mahogany desk with an executive

chair and two flags on poles standing sentinel
to either side. A picture of the governor was
centered in between the poles. Two smaller-
scale leather chairs nestled up to the desk. A
sofa and table with a bronze statue of a bull
rider on a bull were on the other side of the
room. Meg and Stephanie took the leather
chairs across the sheriff's desk. Wyatt stood
a few feet behind Meg's chair, arms crossed,
leaning against the wall.

"I wish I could remember more about the
man who attacked me. I'm just so glad everything turned out okay." Stephanie's shoulders
seemed set in a forward slump. She shot another apologetic look at Meg as more tears
welled.

"You were brave today. Without you, this
could've turned out very differently," Wyatt
said, and there was admiration in his otherwise tight voice. It was probably easier for
him to sympathize with Stephanie, or anyone
who wasn't Meg considering the bomb she'd
dropped on him.

He put his hand on Meg's shoulder and she
ignored the sensual zing of electricity that
always came with his touch. After a year, it
hadn't dimmed and that caught her off guard.

She'd had the same reaction in the parking lot of the restaurant but was too stressed to acknowledge it.

"Mr. Daron, the park worker, gave the sketch artist very little to work with, so we're hopeful his build will seem familiar to one of you." Sawmill picked up a folder on top of a stack of papers on his desk. He showed them the sketch.

Stephanie balked. "He could be half the town. I wouldn't be able to pick him out of a lineup if he was standing right in front of me and I actually knew what he looked like."

Meg stared at the image. It was like a bomb exploded in her brain and yet she had no idea why. She could feel Sawmill's eyes on her, examining her. The blast from the past nearly crippled her. She remembered being in this very office, although the furniture was different then. There had been a different person in the chair opposite her and an overenthusiastic rookie investigator grilling her for answers.

A scared ten-year-old had sat in the chair in Meg's place. Being here, sitting in this very spot caused a lot of bad memories to crash down around her.

Meg took in a fortifying breath. She was no longer an innocent kid being railroaded by a system that too often protected criminals' rights more than victims'. Besides, she'd grown into a woman. Everything in her life had changed since then.

The baby stirred in her arms and looked like she was winding up to cry. Like a balloon deflating, she blew out a breath and made a sucking noise before settling into her mother's arms again.

Meg forced the old thoughts out of her mind—thoughts that had her feeling vulnerable and alone.

"I don't know. Nothing about him looks familiar at all and yet I feel like I should know who he is." She scooted closer to the image, but Sawmill was already up and coming around his desk with the paper in hand.

She took the drawing from him and studied it. Her brain hurt from thinking so hard and she was coming up empty. "All I'm getting is a headache."

But then Stephanie had been the one with Aubrey when she'd been taken. She turned to her friend. "Does he look familiar to you?"

"You've never seen him before?" Sawmill said to Meg, a hauntingly similar note of disappointment in his voice. He had been hoping for better news, based on his tone.

Meg pushed but nothing came except more pain that felt a lot like a brain cramp. "I'm sorry."

Sawmill turned to Stephanie. "What about you, Ms. Gable? Do you know anyone with a similar shape or build?"

She was already shaking her head before he finished his question. "No, sir. Not one person in particular."

"Do you have any idea what age he might be?" Wyatt asked.

"Twenty-five to forty-five," the sheriff supplied.

Not exactly reassuring.

"There must be more to go on than that," Wyatt said. All signs of his casual swagger were gone, replaced by chiseled facade.

"White, male," the sheriff added.

"What about the hair ribbon?" Meg asked, hoping for some good news. "Is it connected to the case?"

"There's no information from forensics yet, ma'am. It might take a few weeks. I called in a favor to see if the results can be fast-tracked. The town's been through enough already without citizens feeling like their families are no longer safe here." The flash of frustration was quickly replaced by determination.

Meg studied the image on the paper in front of her. Fear rippled through her. But why? What was it about him? Was it the fact that this man had tried to kidnap her daughter? Those words were like gut punches.

There was something hauntingly familiar about the outline of his face. But Meg was certain she'd never seen this man before...

Right?

Chapter Four

One look from the sheriff and Meg had to fight her instincts to draw away from him. That look, that same damn look of disappointment bore down on her.

Did he think she wanted the maniac who'd tried to kidnap her daughter to go free?

It made her sick to think this person could try again with another unwitting mother.

Based on his expression, he felt the same way. Another crime in his town, under his nose. They were racking up and she could see every stress crack in the dark circles cradling his eyes. But she also knew in her heart that he couldn't help her or her baby.

Wyatt's eyes were different. His were harder to read than the sheriff's. Hesitation? Yes... well, maybe. Skepticism? Certainly. And something else she couldn't make out. Or, more accurately, didn't have the heart to try. Because it was disappointment in *her*.

Seeing that look in Wyatt's eyes would crush her. And how stupid was that? They'd had a fling and Aubrey was the product. Meg couldn't imagine life without her baby now that she was here, but she hadn't exactly planned for any of this and was still winging the whole parenting thing.

"Mind taking one last look at the sketch?" the sheriff asked Stephanie, and Meg was grateful he'd redirected his attention.

Instinctively, she held her daughter a little closer to her chest, grateful this day hadn't been much worse. Just the thought of anything happening to Aubrey...

No, Meg couldn't go there. Not even hypothetically. Another pang of guilt struck like a physical blow because this whole scenario was too close to home. She had been ten years old when her best friend was abducted right before her eyes and Meg wasn't able to remember a single detail. It had changed her life.

In this case, Meg was the mother who'd almost...*almost*...lost her child. A fresh sense of shame for not being able to bring peace to Mary

Jane's family washed over her, threatening to drag her to the ocean floor.

If only she'd been able to remember what had happened. Mary Jane's family would have the closure that Meg could never give them. She'd seen the Fjords a handful of times after Mary Jane's body had turned up. They'd seemed... *hollow.*

Mary Jane's older brother, Jonathon, had been so affected that he'd had to be pulled out of school and, if memory served, he'd been too traumatized to return. She'd heard rumors that he was homeschooled after because he couldn't bring himself to leave the house.

After this experience of almost losing her own daughter, Meg could certainly understand the Fjords taking extreme measures to keep their son safe. Icy fingers gripped her spine thinking about the past.

All Meg wanted to do was take her baby home and shut out the rest of the world until she could stop trembling.

"I understand the work you do puts you in a precarious situation with folks." Sawmill seemed to realize that continuing to ask her or Stephanie to recognize the kidnapper from barely a sketch was as productive as squeezing water from a cell phone. Meg appreciated the redirection. "Have either of you had any disagreements with clients or been threatened in any way recently?"

Stephanie issued a grunt as Meg shot him a look.

"We help women and children leave abusive households, Sheriff. Being cursed at and threatened comes with the territory," she said.

He nodded and pressed his lips together in a look of solidarity.

"Does a particular incident stand out in your mind?" he asked, and there was a hint of respect in his voice.

"Are you saying this might be personal?" Meg asked. The case she would be testifying for in two weeks had been her main focus since having the baby.

"I wouldn't be doing justice to this investigation if I didn't come at this from every angle," he defended.

He had a point.

"I'm working a case involving a ten-year-old. Kaylee Garza has been physically abused by her soccer-coach father, Randol Garza. It's a typical abuse story in that the little girl has become a master at covering her bruises for school." She looked up at the sheriff in time to see his jaw clench. Hearing about abuse was never easy, especially when it involved children.

Out of the corner of her eye, she also saw that Wyatt's body language was intense. Lines creased his forehead, and tension brackets formed around his mouth. Any decent man wouldn't take hearing what she was about to say lightly and he seemed to know what was coming. She wondered if he'd been subject to abuse as a child and that's what made him seem so sympathetic now. "That is until he whipped her with a cord and she couldn't sit down in class. The domineering father had been abusive to the mother and child for a few years. But this time, he went too far and Kaylee's mother, Virginia, reached out to us for protection and legal help."

"I'm familiar with that story. One of my deputies arrested Mr. Garza. I don't mind saying we were shocked. He seemed like a decent man. Reverend Dawson spoke up on his behalf," the sheriff admitted. "I didn't realize that case was one of yours."

"Garza is fighting the charges against him, and—" she glanced at the sheriff "—he has a lot to lose if Kaylee and her mother's claims turn out to be justified, which they will."

The sheriff stared at her for a long moment. "He coaches the reverend's daughter on that team."

"That's right. There are a few prominent members of the community who have daughters who play for him, as well. Doesn't mean he didn't beat his daughter so hard there were blood blisters on her bottom and legs. Her mother has fallen down the stairs or into a cabinet five times in the past eighteen months, which makes her one the clumsiest people alive or a victim. Given that she was once captain of her college long-distance track team, I seriously doubt she has issues with coordination."

The sheriff leaned back in his chair, examining her as though he was checking her sanity or truthfulness. "My office is aware of the claims."

Hearing about and being witness to such abuses, especially with children, was by far the most difficult part of Meg's job. She couldn't allow herself to focus on that side of the equation for too long or it would be crippling. The bright spot—the good that she would cling to in situations like these—was how much Kaylee and Virginia's lives were going to change. Meg had a chance to guide them to a better future and a more fulfilled life. She couldn't erase their pain, but she could give them the blueprint for their future. In her five years of working for One Child—One Advocate that was the part that kept her going, kept her fighting even when a case seemed hopeless.

"One of your deputies is married to Alysa Estacado," Meg fired back. "She's Garza's cousin. My client asked for this case to be handled by another law enforcement agency and we petitioned the judge on her behalf."

"Mrs. Garza had a tough upbringing. Seems I remember there were drinking problems in her family," Sawmill said.

"If you're saying what I think you are, yes. My client has had her difficulties with alcohol. She's sober now and ready to work," Meg defended.

The sheriff seemed to be contemplating what she said. She could see the road ahead with this case was going to be difficult based on his re-action to the allegations and her client's history. She could only pray the case would be moved, as requested. It was a challenge she accepted with open arms because she could make a difference in Kaylee's life. She could give Virginia a fresh start so she could be the mother she said she wanted to be. Fighting for that was worth every sideways stare she got from people—from the reverend to the sheriff himself.

"I'm not trying to convince you of the merits of this case," she finally said.

Sawmill hesitated like he was about to say something, but his lips thinned and he nodded. "Any other cases I should be aware of?"

She didn't have the heart to defend any more of her clients, considering only the most difficult-to-prove cases ended up on her doorstep. "I'll send a list of names who might be worth investigating."

"I'll need more than that. I want histories, too. I'm especially interested in the past few months. Anyone you think might have a vendetta against you or Ms. Gable," he said. "There's a possibility someone targeted your child in order to show you what it would feel like to have your baby ripped from your arms."

More icy fingers gripped her spine at the suggestion somehow her work was putting her daughter in danger. A scary thought struck. Could Wyatt use that in court to take Aubrey away from her?

Would he?

"I'll email the list with as much detail as I can provide as soon as I get home. I don't have to remind you everything I share is confidential." This was over. Aside from the fact that she had nothing else to contribute, he had already given up on her ability to help. Besides, what happened earlier most likely didn't have anything to do with her current caseload. She'd barely been back to work since having the baby.

There'd been threats before and they were idle. She was always quick to point out to the abusers that if anything happened to her they would be the first stop for the sheriff.

A little voice in the back of her head said that this time no one was threatening. Someone had taken action and they'd done it while the baby was with Stephanie, which would make it harder to tie the crime back to revenge against Meg.

If Meg didn't know any better, she'd get excited about the possibility of forensic evidence nailing the kidnapper. She knew enough to realize that, unlike crime shows on TV, forensics wasn't the be-all and end-all answer for most crimes. Furthermore, it took time to process a crime scene. She could only pray that this whole episode was random and that the attacker would be caught before he could make an attempt on another innocent child.

Meg wanted, no, needed to take her baby home. She stood. She knew the drill, so she preempted the sheriff. "If I can think of anything else, I'll call."

Wyatt caught her arm as she walked toward the door. "Where are you going?"

"Home. Let's go," she said with a finality that he should know better than to argue against.

One glance at him said he fully understood. He released his grip, and she didn't stop walking until they made it into the lobby. Facing the sea of journalists out there looking for a story wasn't exactly her idea of reducing stress.

"Maybe we could huddle together and shield the baby," she said to Stephanie.

"Hold on a minute," Wyatt argued. "What do you think you're doing?"

"Walking out the front door," she said slowly, like she was talking to a two-year-old.

"I can see that. The question is why?" Something about Wyatt made her want to stick around and tell him what was going on. Was it a look? His body language? The sympathy she believed she saw in his eyes?

"Because I can tell when I've lost a battle," she said with a little more heat than she'd intended. "There's nothing else we can do or say in there."

He stood for a long moment in what seemed like a dare. The first one to move lost.

Wyatt took in a sharp breath, a concession breath. "Fine. Let me take you and the baby out the back way to avoid media attention."

Meg held her ground. Her heart thundered against her rib cage as Wyatt disappeared into the sheriff's office. He returned a few seconds later as a deputy motioned for her to follow him toward the opposite hall.

"I'll grab the truck, circle the block and pick you up." Wyatt was a study in determination. His outer appearance was calm, too calm. There was a raging storm swirling beneath the surface and Meg didn't have the energy to withstand the gale-force winds. Not tonight.

Emotions torpedoed through her so fast that she didn't have time to process them. Aubrey was stirring and she didn't want her little girl to pick up the tension in her mother when Wyatt spoke.

Before she could agree or argue, he disappeared. He was probably trying to help, but she didn't need someone walking into her life and taking over. She could think for herself and he needed to see that she'd been fine on her own and especially if the two of them could end up in a courtroom someday.

They could talk in the morning when she had a better perspective and time to gather her thoughts. Meg never fared well when she was caught off guard. She needed to mull things over because all her best decisions came out of respecting her need for time to process information.

As Wyatt walked away she turned to the deputy. "Can you take us home?"

He hesitated and then nodded before leading them out the back and to his SUV. Meg buckled up and held on to Aubrey.

Stephanie flashed eyes at Meg and asked under her breath, "What are you doing?"

"Taking my daughter home," she said plainly.

"What about him?" Stephanie motioned toward the truck that was now behind them.

"Aubrey comes first. She needs to eat, and both he and I need a minute to cool down. There's been a lot thrown at both of us today and we need time to process everything before we make an attempt to figure this out," she said.

"Does that mean he's planning to stick around?" Stephanie's brow went up.

"I have no idea what his plans are. He accused me of trying to use Aubrey to get at the Butler fortune." The accusation still stung and she hadn't had time to process the fact that he was a Butler.

"What does he have to do with the Butlers?" Stephanie didn't hesitate.

"Turns out he's one of them but he didn't seem happy about it," Meg said. A self-made man like Wyatt wouldn't care about the money. The family had been through a lot of trauma since Mr. Butler's murder. The eldest Butler, a female, had been attacked. Another person, Madelyn Kensington, had been summoned to town by the family lawyer in order to be told Mike Butler was her father. A jealous ex had followed Madelyn and nearly killed her. And one of the Butler twins, Dade, had gotten involved with a local woman who barely survived a stalker.

"That family has certainly had their troubles. But he couldn't have meant what he said to you," Stephanie said.

"What makes you so sure?"

"Did you see the way he looks at you?"

Her friend was hallucinating if she thought Wyatt had any feelings left for Meg. He'd been clear about enjoying his single life before. Heck, the times she'd slept over at his place she realized he didn't even have two coffee mugs. What person didn't have two coffee mugs? One could be dirty. Meg didn't have the energy to analyze it again. The message had been clear. Wyatt preferred the number one.

The realization had been a good wake-up call for Meg because she'd been starting down a slippery slope of developing actual feelings for the cowboy-turned-restaurant-mogul. What a disaster that would've been.

"I wish someone looked at me like that," Stephanie said under her breath.

Yeah? Wyatt's steel eyes had been serious, intense. Stephanie was probably misreading the situation.

Aubrey yawned before starting to fuss. Meg repositioned her daughter and spoke in a soothing tone.

The deputy pulled onto the parking pad and Meg thanked him for the ride.

Aubrey fussed and fidgeted as Meg climbed

out of the back seat. "Will you deal with him? I need to take care of her. She's hungry and I'm exhausted."

"I'll take care of the cowboy," Stephanie said, and Meg's heart squeezed. Would Wyatt be attracted to Stephanie? She was beautiful. Was Meg seriously jealous of her best—Meg couldn't bring herself to say *only*, but it was true—friend? "Besides, we need to get the cars home. We left them at work, remember?"

"Yes. Right. Thanks." Seeing Wyatt again was throwing Meg for a loop. She buried those unproductive thoughts and darted inside the house before Wyatt could catch up to her.

Inside, she made a beeline for the kitchen to prepare a bottle, which was difficult while trying to soothe a crying baby. Meg had more experience than she cared to think about, and a rogue thought had her wishing for a partner to help. Not just a partner, her mind protested—the child's father. Wow, her thoughts were careening out of control.

Aubrey belted out a cry that made Meg's heart fist.

"You're okay," she soothed, gently bouncing up and down while finagling the formula and the bottle. She couldn't breastfeed and feared that was one hit in what would be a long line of disappointments for her daughter.

Meg also noted that in seeing the cowboy, as Stephanie had called him, again that she longed for ridiculous things like a family and a home. What would she want next? A minivan? A dog?

Where would that leave all the families who depended on her? And where would that leave her heart when the fairy tale didn't come true?

If her own mother could walk out on her and not look back, why would anyone else stick around?

"I HAVE A right to see Meg and her baby," Wyatt insisted. He already realized convincing Meg's friend to let him inside the house was a losing battle and he should walk away, give the situation some breathing room. He could admit to being part bull when he decided to dig his heels in. His were firmly ground this time.

"I'm really sorry. She needs time," Stephanie said.

Arguing wasn't going to do any good, but Wyatt almost laughed out loud at the thought Meg needed time. "How much? Another year?" There was more anger and frustration in his tone than he'd intended.

Stephanie shrugged.

"She's already had…what?…nine months, plus the baby is how old? How much more time does she need," he countered, clinging to his sinking ship. Wyatt didn't normally lose his cool. He'd built a million-dollar chain of taco stands because of his ability to make good decisions under pressure. As much as he tried to convince himself this was no different, he failed.

Another helpless shrug came from Stephanie.

The timer he'd set on his phone beeped. If he didn't get going he'd miss his meeting with the Butler family. He was tempted to walk away from all of this, from all of Cattle Barge, and never look back. Hell, he had enough on his plate as it was with the expansion of his taco chain. His intention in Cattle Barge had been simple. Put to rest once and for all the fact that he wanted nothing to do with being a Butler, and maybe have a little hot sex with an old flame. Okay, since he was baring his soul, he wanted to have a lot of hot sex with the woman he couldn't seem to keep out of his thoughts in the past year. But that was about as realistic as getting water from a rock. Or, in this case, walking inside that house.

Seeing Meg hold a baby—potentially his baby—should've been a bucket of ice water on the fire between them. Should've been. He was scratching his head as to why that didn't seem to be the case.

"She has my cell. If I don't hear from her in the next few hours I'm coming back and I'm walking inside that door," he warned.

"Understood." Stephanie's hands came up, palms out, in the surrender position. "Like I said before I'm sorry for my friend. I think we've all had a rough morning and need a little time to calm down and sort this mess out."

Since pressuring Stephanie for answers was as smart and productive as firing the guy who runs the cash register because the girl on the line messed up, he decided to cut his losses.

"Fine. I'll be back," he said, realizing it came off more as a threat than a promise.

Wyatt stalked to his truck and took his seat, white-knuckling the steering wheel.

Next up?

Deal with the Butlers.

Wyatt would thank Stephanie for her help when he returned. After all, it wasn't her fault he was in this predicament, and he didn't need to take his frustration out on her. He could've done a better job handling his emotions when talking to Meg. There were a few words he'd take back if he could in hindsight.

In his defense, this situation was emotionally charged without the attempted kidnapping. This also made him wonder if Meg and her baby were safe. He scanned the area. There weren't many houses on this stretch of farm road. He'd been grateful for his truck, given the drive in. Stretches of road needed maintenance. Maybe he could convince Meg to move closer to town when she was thinking straight again. Being closer to supplies and conveniences would be better for her and the baby.

Whoa. Where'd all that come from?

Where Meg chose to live with her daughter was her business. The little girl in the house had gotten to him. He could admit it. Even though he still wasn't ready to believe she was his child, she seemed like a good baby. A sweet helpless little thing. She'd done nothing to provoke a criminal to rip her out of Stephanie's arms. Something had been bugging him since leaving the sheriff's office. The sheriff seemed intent on Meg, but the baby had been taken from Stephanie. What was going on with Sawmill?

If the attempt was related to the kind of work she did—and that was a logical possibility—why not take the baby from Meg, instead? Or had the person been targeting Stephanie? Considering Meg and Stephanie lived under the same roof, it was at least possible that a person could mistake the baby as Stephanie's. *Right?*

Heck, the two lived and worked together so the person could be targeting either of them, based on the work they did.

A rogue thought struck him harder than a sucker punch. Did someone know the baby might be a Butler? Who inside Meg's circle knew about their circumstances? There were a lot of unanswered questions and he was frustrated that his access to Meg was being blocked.

She was trying to protect her daughter, a voice in the back of his mind reminded. He'd seen that fierce look of determination in her eyes, the fire. Justly so. Her daughter was innocent in all this and couldn't exactly fight for herself.

Anger brewed under the surface as he thought about the kind of jerk who abducted little babies. Thinking about how helpless an infant was got all his protective instincts flaring. That's probably what was bugging him the most about this situation and not that he gave any credence to the fact that the little bean shared his DNA.

Until he had definitive proof he wouldn't put too much stock in the idea. Keeping a cool head when everyone else overreacted was another one of his core strengths. He'd call on every skill that had made him the successful man he was today in order to help Meg and her baby while keeping the situation in perspective.

Since patience wasn't one of those skills, he used Bluetooth to call the number on the for-rent sign he'd memorized next door to Meg's place.

Chapter Five

Wyatt leaned forward in his chair, resting his elbows on his knees while waiting for the rest of the Butlers to arrive. He balled one of his hands and gripped it with the other. His thoughts kept drifting toward Meg, her child and the attempted abduction.

An unsettled feeling had gripped him since visiting the sheriff's office and he felt oddly off balance.

Every attempt to bring his thoughts to the present pushed him onto an endless loop. Meg. Baby. Butlers.

He hoped like hell the three weren't connected but couldn't ignore the possibility. Would someone abduct the little girl and then demand ransom?

As much as he'd tried not to care about the Butler family's personal business, they'd been all over the news lately. Living in Texas, he couldn't escape hearing about them or Maverick Mike since his death.

Driving up to the ranch, he was conflicted. He didn't want to like the place. The main building looked like an oversize log cabin. It had a high-end Western-resort feel. And, dammit, he did like it.

A housekeeper led him a short walk down a hall to the dining room. He took a seat, waiting for the rest of the bunch to arrive.

The Solo cup filled with the dark brew he'd picked up on his way over sat on the table. The room itself was decorated to the nines. A long table sat dead center in the room. It looked like one of those hand-carved jobs. A family photo covered the back wall. In the picture, everyone wore jeans and white shirts. They looked to be out on the front lawn. Maverick Mike was in the center and his children flanked his sides. They were younger, maybe early teens, and their father wore a collared shirt along with a white Stetson.

If Wyatt had his druthers, he would be in non-Butler territory for this meeting, a neutral location like the restaurant from lunch. Was that really only seven hours ago? A world of change had happened since then.

"There was something on the news about an attempted kidnapping at the tree-lighting ceremony," the Butler female he recognized as Ella said as she entered the room.

Wyatt stood as twins Dade and Dalton strolled in behind her. Neither commented about this being the first crime in months that didn't have to do with a Butler, so he didn't mention the possibility even though it hovered in a dark corner of his mind.

"I'm Ella," she said to Wyatt as she offered a handshake. Her voice was unreadable, although he'd fully expected a chilly greeting.

He took the offering.

The twins introduced themselves next. They were tall, around Wyatt's height, and he couldn't ignore the fact they shared the same steel eyes and nose as him. Another female entered. She introduced herself as Madelyn Kensington—but he figured she should say Butler—as she took the seat next to his. Solidarity?

Spare him.

Had the seating been arranged on purpose, putting the other bastard Butler next to him in order to make him feel a sense of kinship? Put the two outsiders together so they could form a bond. No, thanks.

Wyatt positioned his body toward Ella, who was chatting easily with her newfound sister. Wasn't that cozy?

One of the twins acknowledged Wyatt with a sharp nod. Anger. That was more Wyatt's speed.

The family lawyer walked in, taking a seat on the other side of Wyatt. Cozy.

"Thank you for coming today," Ed Staples said after a formal introduction.

"You already know I'm only here because you summoned me," Wyatt informed the group as he looked toward the lawyer.

A few exchanged glances.

"Mr. Jackson has made his position clear," Ed reiterated to the group. "It took some convincing to get him to show today."

"I'd appreciate getting down to the reason for this meeting," Wyatt said to Ed.

"We're waiting for one more person," Ed responded.

Wyatt glanced around. How many more Butlers did they need to have a meeting? As it was, he felt surrounded by them, and an unfamiliar feeling of claustrophobia edged its way in. His chest started feeling tight and oxygen was in short supply.

He checked the time on the screen of his cell phone, chalking up part of his reaction to being away from Meg and not knowing if everything was okay on her end. "With all due respect, I have other business."

"I'll get my sister." Ella flashed her eyes at him. "*Our* sister, Cadence, on the phone."

"I'm an only child," Wyatt said through clenched teeth. He was ready for an argument, but none came. In fact, he was pretty damn sure one of the twins had just winked at the newest member of the Butler clan, Madelyn. Ignoring the protests rising up in his chest, he palmed his phone and checked his in-box. There were 1,256 emails. His email had blown up overnight. He used his thumb to scroll through the names, swirling around in his chair until his back was to the dinner table.

Wyatt had arguably one of the best poker faces in Texas, but his emotions were in high gear with the whole him-maybe-being-someone's-father bomb that had been dropped in the last twelve hours. He was distracted. His mind wasn't on business or the Butlers, and especially not this meeting.

Being here was a bad idea.

He skimmed a few key emails. Construction on the new location where they'd just broken ground had been stopped by the city. Crews had been sent home, and without the proper permits a nice chunk of money that Wyatt had already spent would be for nothing. Granted, he didn't need the cash. But if he couldn't get this project off the ground a lot of jobs would be compromised and people would be out of work. He'd already hired most of the staff for the new taco restaurant and they were training in Houston so they could get up and running on day one, which was supposed to happen in seven weeks. What was he supposed to tell them? They no longer had jobs because the city changed its mind?

This location had been strategically chosen because the rubber plant that had given half the town jobs was closing down. Wyatt believed in creating jobs in small communities so families could stay intact and small dots on the map where people had lived for generations wouldn't end up ghost towns in a few years when all the young people had to move to a bigger city for work. He and his mother had moved around a lot before settling in Austin where she waited tables. During his childhood, they'd always returned to a lake house near Bay. He was never sure how his mother had pulled it off, but every year no matter how difficult their circumstances were they'd spent a week there during the summer.

There was something extra special about Bay, Texas. Bringing his successful business there to give reasonable-paying jobs to people—unlike when his mother worked for the rubber plant—meant more than it should. He knew better than to mix business with emotion, and now it was coming back to bite him. And especially since he'd decided to look into buying the place where he and his mother had built so many happy memories.

A better business location would be to stay southwest, where he already had friendly politicians who appreciated him bringing work to their constituents.

Thinking with the beating heart in his chest instead of his hard-won intelligence was proof that he was losing his edge. He deserved the backlash.

Another troubling email caught his attention.

His lawyer said no one owned the house in Bay by the lake. It was owned by a conglomerate in the Cayman Islands. All that said to Wyatt was that some CEO, probably a wealthy guy in Houston, was using his company to shield ownership of the house on the water. Fine. Dealing with a businessman was much easier than a new mother. In that arena, he knew exactly what he was doing.

He excused himself into the hallway and made a quick call to his lawyer, Alexander Kegel.

"I got your email about the Bay property," Wyatt said after perfunctory greetings.

"How do you want to proceed?" his lawyer asked.

"Find out who the company belongs to and which CEO is hiding behind it. Once you do, I need to find out what's important to him or her." Business was all about finding the right leverage.

"Done. I'll have a report to you in the morning," Alexander said.

Wyatt thanked his lawyer as he heard a voice coming through what sounded like a speaker in the room behind him. He turned to find five sets of eyes on him.

"Ready?" Ed Staples asked.

"Let's get on with it," one of the twins said, and his words were like fingernails on a chalkboard to Wyatt. Did he have any idea how little Wyatt wanted to be in this room with all of them? Clearly, the answer was no.

His skin itched being inside Maverick Mike Butler's home staring at four people who looked so similar. They had the same nose as their father, and Wyatt had instantly realized it was like staring at his own. It was all a little too close to home for his comfort. He wanted to know what Meg was doing.

"I'm not sure why I let you talk me into coming here." Wyatt looked squarely at Ed Staples. "I don't want any of this."

With that, he walked down the hall and through the front door. He heard the click of boots on tile behind him, but he didn't stop to find out who they belonged to.

"Hold up a minute." It was one of the twins.

Wyatt stopped but didn't turn to find out which one had followed him. He didn't care.

"Look, I know my, *our*, father didn't do the right thing when he was alive, but—"

"Save it." Wyatt whirled around, staring

into eyes that looked a little too much like his own. Déjà vu from earlier, from being with Aubrey, assaulted him. His sour mood intensified.

The guy's hand came up. "I won't pretend that I know what this must be like for you because I don't. I grew up with the man and, until recently, had the same look you do when anyone brought him up."

At least the guy was smart enough not to go down the road of wondering why Wyatt didn't want to be there. That eased a little of the tension stringing Wyatt's shoulders so taut they might snap. Business was responsible for at least part of his high strung emotions. But his thoughts also kept rounding back to Meg and that little girl.

"I'm sorry for how this has all played out," Dade said.

Wyatt listened mostly because he didn't want to come off as a jerk with someone who'd done nothing wrong. The man's father was a whole other story.

"Why not listen to what Ed has to say? Whatever feelings you have toward our—" he glanced at Wyatt and seemed to decide to change his tack "—toward Maverick Mike have nothing to do with him."

Wyatt's brow shot up as anger burned his chest.

"Really? Isn't he here to speak to me on behalf of the man who walked out on my mother, leaving her to fend for herself?" Saying those words out loud hit him like a sucker punch to the gut. Was that what he'd done to Meg? Was doing?

This was different. She'd pushed him away. He'd been more than willing to stick around and do whatever was necessary to pitch in until this whole ordeal was sorted out.

"We're not trying to mess with you. We have no idea what the old man wanted to say, but it might not be his fault that your mother lived the way she did."

Those words were gasoline on a fire. There was no way his mother wanted to live in poverty, paycheck to paycheck, with no medical insurance and no security. No one could convince him that she didn't want to be able to load the Christmas tree with presents every year instead of relying on the kindness of strangers through a church program. He was grateful—don't get him wrong—but his mother would never have chosen the life they'd lived if she'd had another option. Sure, she was a proud woman. But there was nothing empowering about standing in line in twenty-degree weather during a cold snap on Thanksgiving morning in order to get a plate of turkey.

"I don't need any of this in my life. I'm done." Wyatt swept his hand across the air.

"That's understandable under the circumstances," Dade admitted. "But my father has surprised us more than once recently. He might have something to offer you, too."

"No. I don't care about him. I don't need anything from him or any of you," Wyatt managed to get out through clenched teeth.

"Then by all means walk away." Dade started to turn.

For reasons Wyatt couldn't explain, he shouted, "I don't want his money, either."

"Neither do I," Dade countered. "But you know, life sometimes deals one helluva punch and you might just need a family to lean on."

"I've done all right by myself so far," Wyatt ground out, thinking Dade was sorely misguided if he thought Wyatt needed a Butler to make his life complete. Meg came to his mind, but he quickly shot down that idea as mental treason. He had a successful business to occupy his time, more money than he could spend and a beautiful home in the hills outside of Austin along with several other homes in Texas. What more could any man ask for?

Did he have regrets? Sure.

"Then you don't need to stick around." Dade was walking a thin line. Wyatt thought about hooking a right fist over that left eye of his.

But what did he care?

Wyatt wasn't now, nor would he ever be, a Butler. It was time to walk away.

MEG WAS UP before the sun. She thought about the list of names she'd sent the sheriff yesterday, hoping she'd covered every threat. Wyatt had stopped by again last night, but Meg had been sleeping so Stephanie left a note on her bathroom door—a note that Meg had read at two o'clock in the morning. Even then, her heart pounded thinking about him. She was tired and that was causing her to lose her mind.

The Garza case needed her attention, but focus on work seemed as attainable as a hundred-carat diamond necklace.

Thankfully, Aubrey was already fed and

back to sleep. At two-months-old her routine consisted of feed, sleep, repeat.

Looking down at her little girl, she couldn't be upset about the amount of work an infant brought. Even facing Wyatt and delivering the life-changing news to him had paled in comparison to the horror of Aubrey being abducted.

Yesterday had been the worst day of Meg's life. She couldn't even begin to process the thought of her baby disappearing forever. Hot tears burned the backs of her eyes.

Coffee.

She needed coffee.

She wiped the moisture from her eyes and stalked toward the kitchen with one mission: caffeine.

Before she took her first sip of fresh brew, Stephanie sauntered into the kitchen and poured herself a cup of coffee. Her hair looked like a lion's mane, thick and golden. The waves highlighted her friend's heart-shaped face and suited her.

"What time did you get the little sprig to sleep last night?" Stephanie asked Meg.

"It's all a blur." Aubrey came into the world weighing almost seven pounds and seemed determined to bulk up. The little angel ate almost every two hours on the nose—still. Meg had learned that she was far less conscious of losing sleep when she had no idea how much she was losing. "Been up on and off since then. How about you? How'd you sleep? I tried my best not to wake you."

"Me? I slept like a log. You must be exhausted after yesterday. I'd offer to take her out this morning so you could get some sleep, but I'm scared after what happened." Stephanie wasn't the type to back down from many things, so her attitude caught Meg off guard.

"That wasn't your fault," Meg reassured. "I know you would never do anything to put her in harm's way."

"Thank you. But she was with me when it happened. Of course, I feel responsible. If anything happened to her, I'd never forgive myself." Stephanie wiped at her eye and Meg figured she was swiping away a tear. She gave her friend some space.

"You're a good friend and the best aunt she'll ever have," Meg said.

"I'm her only aunt," Stephanie said through a half laugh, half sniff. At least she sounded lighter than a moment ago. Meg wouldn't allow her friend to shoulder the burden of some random creep trying to take Aubrey.

The thought gave Meg chills.

"I still can't believe you came home, fed her and worked out." Stephanie faced her and took a sip of coffee.

Meg gripped her mug. "Guess I just wanted to feel like something was normal again. Like I had some control of my routine."

"Did you remember anything about the sketch the sheriff showed us?" Stephanie asked and Meg shot a look. "Never mind. I can see by your reaction that you didn't. I'm in the same boat."

Talking about the sheriff's office brought more tension to Meg's already tight shoulders. Working out had given her a speck of normalcy last night. Maybe discussing work, like they always did over their first cups of coffee, would do the same. "What about the Barber case? Did you get a chance to review the files I sent last week?"

"Not yet. I haven't wrapped up the St. James case," Stephanie admitted.

"What's going on with that one?" Meg asked.

"Looks like he might get off with probation,"

she said on a sigh. They didn't win justice for every case they took on.

"It's important that our clients know someone cares about them. We can still get them the help they need to change their lives even if the courts give him a free pass," Meg reminded. She could see the defeat in her friend's eyes. Neither one of them took losing easily and that's probably why they both fought so hard for people.

"He's basically getting a slap on the wrist." Stephanie made eyes at Meg.

"This time. If he messes up with someone else it won't be the same. He has a record now. He won't get off so easily if he pulls anything like this in the future and that's an important win."

Stephanie rocked her head in agreement. "True."

"You made a difference for Adrien and her daughters. Now we can give them the right tools to help break the cycle so they'll have better lives." When Meg took a hit on a case, Stephanie made it her job to pump Meg up and vice versa.

"You're right." Stephanie offered a weak smile, but it was better than nothing. "I'll do a workup on services we can connect Adrien to so that she and the girls can get on their feet."

Meg was grateful to talk about work for a change instead of the haunting image of someone trying to rip her daughter out of her arms. She walked over to the front door. "Did you check the mail yesterday?"

"I forgot after all that happened," Stephanie said.

"I'll do it." Meg opened the door and walked onto the small porch. She glanced across the street and saw something she wasn't ready to deal with this early in the morning, Wyatt's truck. She jumped back inside, closed and locked the door. "What's he doing here?"

"Who? Where?" Stephanie glanced around like she half expected someone to be standing in the kitchen next to her.

"Wyatt's truck is parked across the street." Meg searched for her cell. Where had she put it last night?

Stephanie checked the window for herself.

"At the empty house," Meg provided.

"That one used to be for rent." Stephanie checked out the window and gasped when her suspicion seemed to be confirmed. "Where'd the sign go?"

"What did he say last night?" Meg asked as she continued to unearth pillows, looking for the electronic device that held every important contact she had.

"That he wasn't finished and planned to stick around until you spoke to him," she said.

"You didn't put that on the note." Meg moved to the chair and dug her hands in the seam between the cushion and the armrest. Panic assaulted her.

"Figured I'd tell you when I saw you." Stephanie joined her. "What are we looking for?"

"My phone."

"Oh. I saw that on the counter." Stephanie motioned toward the kitchen.

Meg must've set it down when she was in a hurry to make Aubrey's bottle last night.

Before she could find it, a knock sounded at the front door. Her pulse jackhammered against her ribs.

"I'll get it," she said. For a split second, she wondered what she looked like. The thought was ridiculous under the circumstances. She had on yoga pants and a shirt. She ran her hand through her hair to smooth it down.

Meg stalked to the front door and opened it,

thankful she'd had at least one strong cup of coffee before facing Wyatt again.

When she saw him standing there her traitorous heart galloped.

"Meg, this is Dr. Raul. With your permission he'd like to perform a DNA test." Wyatt's expression was stone and his voice gave away nothing. He was steady as steel—just like his eyes—and part of her resented him for being so calm when his presence rattled her to the core.

At least she'd told him about Aubrey. Her secret was out. He deserved to know that he was the little girl's father. And there were so many other issues to deal with rather than obsessing over what his reaction might be today. And yet she was still hurt by his insistence on a DNA test. Was that silly?

What had she expected? Him to take the baby from her arms before getting down on one knee and proposing they become a family?

Right. That was about as smart as dumping acid in the garden and expecting flowers to grow.

"She's sleeping right now, but—"

"There's no need to wake her. I can use a strand of hair from a hairbrush or if you have a recently used bottle available that would work,"

Dr. Raul said. He was a study in compassion with his rounded shoulders and kind expression. He held a bag in his right hand and she could guess the contents included a DNA sampling kit.

"Fine," she responded. "Follow me."

Chapter Six

Meg opened the door and stepped aside to allow them access, ignoring the chill bumps racing up her arms from the burst of cold air. She walked into the kitchen, making eyes at Stephanie so her friend would know to stick around.

Wyatt and the doctor followed her, and she didn't like the way she could feel Wyatt's masculine presence behind her when he seemed so unaffected by her. He didn't say a word as the doctor went to work, gathering the bottle without touching the tip.

"Who's this?" Stephanie asked.

"A doctor. Wyatt wants a paternity test," Meg said as evenly as she could.

Stephanie rolled her eyes. "Does he know you can get a test at the drugstore and be done in ten minutes?"

"I didn't ask," Meg said with a slight smirk.

"Excuse me if I don't want to leave something as important as this to a dime-store test," Wyatt said on a clipped tone.

Meg didn't offer coffee, mainly because she didn't want them to stick around. As it was she had about an hour before it was time to feed Aubrey again, and she wanted to get in a hot morning shower to ease the tension trapped between her shoulder blades.

"And now a swab from Dad," the doctor said. The word *dad* had an unexpected effect on Meg and she started to tear up. She quickly turned her back to them and reached for the coffee-pot. Her reaction most likely stemmed from the fact that she'd never known her own father. He'd ducked out on her and her mother before Meg started school. As much as she didn't want Wyatt to be forced back into her life permanently, she also realized having an attentive father would be best for Aubrey. Based on his reactions so far, when the test came out positive she was going to have to make room for him in her life.

After refilling her mug and getting her over-wrought emotions under control—emotions that had been on shaky ground ever since the pregnancy, thanks to all those hormones—she faced them again.

"Seems like you have everything you need," she said, her gaze bouncing from Wyatt to the doctor to the door. If that wasn't subtle enough, she took in a sharp breath and stared boldly at Wyatt.

"Any chance I can get a cup of coffee before I go?" Wyatt asked, holding her gaze. Another dare?

He'd conceded on the last one and she figured she was going to have to learn how to meet him halfway.

She focused on the doctor. "Coffee?"

"None for me, thanks. I have work to do." Dr. Raul held up the specimens. "I'll call with the results as soon as they come in."

"I'll walk you out," Stephanie piped in, and that was not the kind of help Meg was hoping for. She didn't want to be left alone in the kitchen with Wyatt and she couldn't even pinpoint the reason why. Yes, he unnerved her. No, she didn't think they had anything to talk about until he confirmed what she already knew. He was Aubrey's father. Yet, he wanted to stick around.

After the events of yesterday, maybe he just needed to know she was all right.

Meg poured a fresh cup of hot brew and handed it to him, ignoring the frisson of heat when their fingers grazed. She'd give it to him that he looked good, even better than she'd remembered. But—and it was a big *but*—she'd always known he wasn't the stick-around type, and the news she'd delivered yesterday had clearly knocked him off balance.

Heck, she felt the same way. Life was a lot smoother without overcomplicating it with emotions. Okay, sure hers had already engaged, and that confused her even more at the time. It would be just like her to want to start a relationship with another emotionally unavailable person. If there was a Been There Done That T-shirt for picking the wrong type she'd have a closetful. She'd blame her parents for ditching her—and that might partly be true—but she also took blame where it belonged, which was with her. She didn't want to risk her heart by truly falling for someone. Those lines ran deep within her and, if she had to guess, had started when she was ten-years-old.

The worst part was that she wasn't gullible. On some level she realized that she was choosing unavailable men on purpose and the reason was to give her an escape route. Meg didn't get close to people. Period.

Having a daughter was softening Meg. She'd fallen for that little girl the minute she saw those round cheeks and blue eyes, as clichéd as that might sound. Stephanie was the only other person Meg trusted enough to let inside her carefully constructed walls, and the two of them had only become close recently, after Meg had learned she was pregnant.

Meg thought back to the last real friend she'd had before Stephanie. Mary Jane. Her ten-year-old best friend. A tear escaped just thinking about her.

"Hey, everything okay?" Wyatt asked, and she glanced up at him in time to see that he was studying her intensely.

"Yes," she lied, but then decided to come clean. "No. Not really."

"I apologize if—"

"You have every right to expect proof," she said quickly, not wanting him to spell out his distrust of her. Somehow, that would only make things worse in her mind and this was Aubrey's father. For her daughter's sake, Meg needed to find middle ground with him. "It's a lot to chew at once. I'd probably request the same thing if I was in your shoes."

He started to say something but seemed to think better of it, taking a sip of coffee instead.

She needed to redirect the conversation away from the two of them and all that their relationship lacked. "The sketch kept coming back to me last night and I don't know why. I don't think I've never seen him before." She had to consider the possibility that he was someone from her past that she'd blocked out. But who? Why?

"The person who attempted to take Aubrey yesterday did so while she was with Stephanie," Wyatt said, and she could almost see the pins firing inside his brain. He was an intelligent businessman. He'd learned to look at all angles, and he could probably be a big help if she let him in.

Opening herself up even a crack was so hard. Meg had been rejected by everyone she let in.

She studied Wyatt, debating. "Does that mean you think the kidnapping attempt was random?"

"It's a definite possibility. We didn't ask the sheriff if there'd been any similar cases reported in the area or across Texas," he continued, and she liked the way he was thinking. If this wasn't personal, she and Aubrey could be safer. Meg might not have to check the back seat of every car before she got inside or the closets before she went to bed at night. But then, those were habits she'd developed a long time ago and had never been able to shake.

After yesterday, Meg wondered if she'd ever truly feel safe again. "With the holidays around the corner, I read somewhere that infant abductions are more common."

"People start realizing what's missing in their lives and want to fill the gap. Your daughter is beautiful. Those two facts alone could make her a target," he said. Was there reverence in his voice when he talked about Aubrey? "A sad fact of this time of year is that situations like these happen. People who are desperate to have a child are sometimes willing to pay any price without realizing what that might do to someone else. Some have no idea and don't care how they get a baby, just that they get one."

"How do you know all this?" Had he gone back to the sheriff last night?

"Started searching around on the internet last night when I couldn't sleep," he admitted. "Wanted to figure out a profile of someone capable of this. Thought that maybe I could help move the investigation along if I found the right information."

"Did you call the sheriff?" She couldn't hide her shock.

"Before the sun came up," he admitted.

Meg grunted. She would've liked to have been a fly on that wall. "How'd Sawmill take that phone call?"

Wyatt cocked an eyebrow. "What makes you ask?"

"Most of my cases are outside of Cattle Barge and that's one of the main reasons I live here. I like to keep work and home separate. But I've had a few—"

"Like the Garza one you talked about yesterday?" he asked.

She nodded.

"Most law-enforcement officers have a hard time with people they consider outsiders poking around in their business," she said. "Many already feel they have constant eyes on them, be it citizens complaining or those cameras that both help and hurt them when they record everything that's happening. Being an advocate for victims' rights puts me across the table from law enforcement sometimes."

"Which doesn't faze you," he said, but it came off as more question than statement.

"I've gotten used to being the opposition," she admitted, and maybe that was another way to keep people at arm's length. "Because the people I work on behalf of deserve someone strong sitting across from investigators who may have mishandled an investigation. Or don't deserve to be subject to a law that offers more protection to the guilty person than the victim."

"You're passionate about your work." This time, he was examining her like he was looking at her for the first time, and she didn't want to acknowledge the sensual shivers skittering across her skin or the awareness causing her breath to catch.

She couldn't afford to notice the hint of appreciation in his eyes, either.

"I can't imagine wanting to be a mother so badly that you'd be willing to take a child from someone who loves her. The pregnancy caught me off guard and, believe me, I considered all my options more times than I care to admit. In the end, I decided to keep her—obviously—and hoped that I wouldn't mess up being a mother too badly," she admitted, a little unsure why she'd gone there. She hadn't told a soul about her misgivings about parenting before, and she'd already spilled more about her work to him than she anyone in her past.

But, then, things had changed between them. This was Aubrey's father now. Maybe a piece of her wanted him to get to know her so he wouldn't be tempted to fight her for custody. If he saw how hard she worked and how much she cared for their child he'd be more compassionate.

Because when it came down to money, he had buckets more to spend on lawyers than she did. It also seemed like he was in the same boat since the parenting news had been dropped on him. And maybe that was another reason she started talking. She wished she'd had someone to lean on when her entire life had been turned upside down with the news. Part of her wanted him to know that she'd had a similar reaction.

Or maybe it was selfish and she felt he was the only other person in the world who could truly understand her feelings. They were the only two involved even if they were in different places. They were on opposite sides of the same boat, rowing toward some unknown future.

Aubrey deserved the best both had to offer. There he was, studying her. There was something else in his eyes, too. Something that was familiar. Maybe intimate.

"Whatever else happens," he started, and took a step toward her. Goose bumps sprouted on her arms, and she was very aware of how close they were now. "I know you're an amazing mother. I can see how much you love her and she's lucky because not every kid gets that."

"She's worth it." If she looked into those steel eyes much longer she'd be in even bigger trouble than she already was. Suddenly, the rim of her coffee cup became interesting.

Wyatt took another step toward her and she could see the tips of his boots as she focused on the tile floor. She felt his finger graze her chin as he urged her to look up.

She resisted at first because the heat pinging between them would give away her reaction to him and she didn't want him to know how much her body missed the feel of him, of kissing him, of his weight on top of her while they made love. She took a step back but was stopped by the counter. He followed and by the time she looked up, she could see him angle his head as he brought his lips down to crash against hers.

The second their mouths touched, warning bells sounded, but they were muted by the heat rising between them as his body pressed against hers. There was so much heat in the kiss that she was rendered breathless. Fighting against her feelings was no use when he was this close. Besides, she had wanted this since seeing him again even though she knew better.

He dropped his hand to her waist and made a sexy little grunting noise against her mouth and Meg got lost.

Stephanie cleared her throat in the next room, an obvious attempt to let them know she was coming back.

Wyatt sidestepped and turned around to face her. Meg brought her coffee cup up to take a sip, thinking she liked the way it had tasted on Wyatt's lips a few seconds ago, mixed with his toothpaste. Knowing those thoughts were dangerous.

Kissing him was a mistake, a distraction they couldn't afford. She could feel his presence in every bit of her body, especially as it still hummed with electricity even after they'd broken physical contact.

"The doctor said he'd get the results to you in a couple of hours," Stephanie said to Wyatt. Her voice was curt as she shot a warning look toward Meg. Her friend was watching out for her and Meg was grateful. The last thing she needed was to fall down that slippery slope of having feelings for Wyatt again. He'd been clear that he didn't do long-term from the start.

Perfect, Meg had thought, because neither did she. Her heart had betrayed her, wishing for more than she knew better to expect.

A dull ache started forming between her eyes and she needed ibuprofen. She checked the pantry.

"Are we out of pain relievers?" she asked Stephanie.

"I took the last one yesterday," Stephanie said. "Put them on the list for this week's shopping, which isn't doing you any good right now."

Wyatt stood there cool as he could be with his legs crossed at the ankles and his hip leaning against the counter.

Meg's heart fluttered like a trapped bird.

WYATT NEEDED TO find the brake pedal when it came to his attraction to Meg. Or at least downshift to Neutral. Kissing her was a big-time mistake and he tried to convince himself that it had more to do with all the other things

in his life careening out of control. That it was
a way of getting his hands back on the wheel
and his backside in the driver's seat. A grab-
the-bull-by-the-horns approach to life. Because
that had worked in the past. Anytime he'd had
a hiccup— and there'd been plenty starting a
business from the ground up—he'd faced his
issues head-on.

Case in point, at the end of his first real expansion, when he'd moved to five taco stands,
his manager, Tim McGowan, had decided to
put his hand in the till. Tim had been the closest thing Wyatt had had to a close buddy, which
made the betrayal sting all that more.

Turned out, Tim was selling items without
ringing them up and blaming his employees for
the inventory not matching the register receipts.
Meanwhile, he was pocketing the difference.
The worst part was that Tim was blaming a
sixteen-year-old—a kid he'd hired—for mess-
ing up the balance sheet.

When Wyatt had first been alerted to the
problem, he'd been back at home in Austin
for the first time in six months, staring at an
empty calendar and bed. He'd had the kind of
exhaustion that made his eyelids feel like sand-
paper rubbing against his eyeballs. And nothing

seemed more important than pulling the sheet over his shoulders and hibernating for a solid week to catch up on sleep.

Tim had called to let him know he was checking into a problem that "the kid," as he'd called Dwayne, had noticed. The minute something felt off with Tim, Wyatt didn't hesitate to hop in his truck and head to Brunson Falls. He drove for five hours after filling his truck with gas even though he was personally on an empty tank. Caffeine and pit bull determination to be successful had been his fuel.

When he'd arrived at the Brunson Falls location he immediately knew something was off. Tim acted cagey and made a few inappropriate jokes. Wyatt had trusted a handful of people and Tim was one of them. It was clear to Wyatt now that his judgment had been off.

Trying to dim his attraction to Meg—even now after her out-of-the-blue announcement that he was the father of her child—should've dimmed his attraction to her. Facing it head-on was like pouring gasoline onto a raging fire, and his body was still having a reaction to standing so close to her. He'd blame it on autopilot or muscle memory, but he'd wanted to kiss her and he was a little too aware of the fact.

He grinned as he stared into his coffee cup.
Damn.

Time to refocus.

Locking onto Meg's gaze almost caused him
to rethink what he was about to say. Call it
cowboy code, but he couldn't walk away from
Meg and her daughter while they were in danger. "Whether that kid is mine or not, I'm planning on sticking around until I know you're
both safe."

A flicker of impatience crossed Meg's eyes.
He held up his hand to stop her from speaking.
"I know what you're about to say, and I have
no doubt that you can take care of yourself and
her. Think of me as insurance."

"Is that why you rented the place next door?"
Her bottom lip had a slight pout, the same one
he'd seen before when she was frustrated.

"Yes. And I have other business in Cattle
Barge to address," he added.

Her cheeks were still flushed, her lips still
full and pink. He fisted his free hand to stop
it from reaching out to touch her again. Call it
instinct, habit, muscle memory. Or maybe *stupid* was a better word because he'd learned a
long time ago that touching a hot stove burned
him, and yet there he'd been ready to do it again

with Meg. If Aubrey turned out to be his child, he needed to keep a clear head and oven mitts handy. He had no plans to fan the flame burning between him and Meg.

"The fact that you're a Butler?" Meg asked, and mention of that family went a long way toward that direction.

"I'll never be a Butler," he said low and under his breath. But he might actually be a father. The word caused his blood pressure to rise.

The timing of Aubrey's birth was spot on from when they'd been together. He'd calculated the dates a dozen times last night. They'd been careful, like he always was, but he remembered a pair of times things got so hot and heavy between them neither noticed when the condom broke.

To be fair, either time could've resulted in pregnancy.

"It's a big family," Meg said, cutting into his heavy thoughts. "I've heard good things about them. They do a lot of charitable work in the community and seem like they really want to make a difference in people's lives."

Nothing good could come of his having Maverick Mike Butler as a father. "How well do you really know them?"

"I don't. Just what I've seen in the news and on society pages. They seem to stick together, and I guess I wish Aubrey had that kind of support. All she has is me," she said, and her honesty caught him off guard.

The baby cried from the next room and, before Meg could disappear, Stephanie was bringing the little girl to her mother. Stephanie went to work making a bottle while Meg soothed the infant.

If Aubrey turned out to be Wyatt's daughter, she was going to have a helluva lot more than just Meg for support.

Finances wouldn't be a problem, either. He'd be ready and willing to take care of expenses, put them in a nicer house and newer SUV. His mind was already clicking through other financial needs the girl might have, like braces, dance classes and college.

Money was the easy part. The rest was barbed-wire complicated. Move too fast and the barbs would dig deeper into the skin. Fight against them, get the same result.

Thinking about Maverick Mike Butler, the man who'd donated his sperm, stirred emotions in Wyatt's chest that he didn't want to explore. Something hard, like a stone being tossed at him, nailed his gut every time Wyatt thought about the man.

What kind of father abandoned his own son? His thoughts went to Madelyn.

A dark thought struck. Would history repeat itself, only this time Wyatt would be the jerk dad pulling the disappearing act? Was he doomed by his DNA to be as big a letdown as the senior Butler had been?

The thing that bothered him the most in the past five years was the words his mother had said to him on her deathbed after he'd told her about his expansion plans. She'd beamed up at him with something that looked a lot like pride and said, "You're going to be so successful. Just like your father. You remind me so much of him."

How was that for shooting a lead arrow through his heart?

Wyatt reminded his own mother of the man who'd abandoned them both. Figuring out what that look of pride had been about had cost Wyatt countless nights of sleep, though he wasn't much on sleep when he could be working instead.

Hold on a second. Why was he already clicking through all this in his mind, anyway?

There'd only been a statement, not proof, that the little girl was his.

Was it because deep down he realized that Meg wasn't the type to make a false accusation?

But that was no reason to lose his mind. He needed to think clearly in order to get to the bottom of this.

So, why did that child's eyes haunt him so much?

A little voice said, *Because they belonged to him.*

Chapter Seven

"Before, you said that you were worried about the possibility of Aubrey being targeted due to the Butler name," Meg said, and there was a strained quality to her voice as she watched him. She'd witnessed his entire thought process and it must've played across his face, because she'd stopped feeding the baby and was studying him as she draped the little girl over her shoulder and patted her on the back.

"It crossed my mind. It seems most want a piece of the Butlers these days." Wyatt stood and tried to shake off the heavy thoughts. He needed air and a damn good session at the gym. Since the latter wasn't possible he decided instead to take a few steps away from the situation. All he needed was a fresh perspective, and yet something warned nothing would ever be that easy again. "Can we talk about that later?"

"Okay."

"I can run out. Pick up a bottle of ibuprofen," he offered.

"I'll just get a few dollars," Meg said with a curious glance.

"No need." He threw on his jacket and palmed his keys, impatience edging his tone. Fresh air would do him good. He plugged in the request to his GPS and located the closest store. "Shouldn't take too long. You'll be okay until I get back?"

"We'll be fine." Meg's face muscles were pulled taut, belying her words.

Wyatt walked out the door and climbed into the driver's seat of his truck. The two-bedroom bungalow-style house had many of Meg's personal touches, from the oil-on-canvas painting on the wall she'd told him she was painting last year to the worn-in warm tones in the furniture. The place was just big enough to still be considered cozy, and her kitchen was functional. The place even smelled like her, a mix of lavender and clean and fresh air that was somehow all Meg. He'd never known the difference between lavender and any other herb until he'd asked.

Thinking back to the easy way they had of relating in the past and the white-hot passion in the bedroom brought back other memories, unwanted memories. Like when he'd finally convinced her to sleep over at his place and woke with her in his arms. He'd liked waking up to having a cup of coffee on the balcony of his place overlooking the Austin skyline. And he'd wanted to show her the home that was being built.

But then she'd slowed down and had refused to stay over again. Not long after, he'd wondered if he'd overstepped some invisible boundary with her. It had made him laugh at the time because those thoughts had never crossed his mind before her. He'd reminded himself to get a grip and done his level best to convince himself his feelings weren't hurt when she'd said she was too busy to meet him for dinner the next day.

Hadn't his thoughts derailed?

Wyatt tried to maintain focus on the problems at hand by stuffing his past down deep. He had a media mess brewing with the Butler news threatening to surface at any minute, and he might even enjoy the fireworks his presence seemed to ignite within the famed family if it weren't for the fact that his life was careening out of control.

The announcement of the reading of his father's will on Christmas Eve was another in a long list of things that didn't sit well, and Wyatt had never been a big holiday person.

What he couldn't figure out was...why? Why include him?

In life, the man had never once tried to forge a relationship or help Wyatt's mother in any way. She'd had to live day to day and do without even though she never complained. He'd seen it in the worry lines in her forehead and the way she often paced while figuring out finances. Growing up watching his mother trapped in a powerless situation built a lot of residual anger in a kid, in a man.

He'd used it to fuel his need to be a success on his own even more. He'd developed an amazing ability to shut out the world and zero in on one thing—success.

As his first taco restaurant reached its major success milestone, his mother was barely clinging to life. He'd been in the process of buying a proper house for her as a surprise. She'd been sick for a while but hadn't told him about the terminal diagnosis until the very end, leaving him with tremendous guilt for not spending time with her.

He'd built a successful food franchise on his own and had no plans now or ever to lower himself to the point of getting in line for a piece of the Butler estate. He would never give the man or his family the satisfaction of thinking that he needed them in any way.

A fifteen-minute drive on underdeveloped roads made him appreciate his truck even more. He thought about Meg's older model SUV. It was good enough to get by for now. She'd need something newer with recent safety features. That was an easy fix. She must like the model she owned or she wouldn't have bought it. He'd order the latest and have it delivered.

The convenience store was on the corner of one too many farm roads if anyone asked Wyatt. He also noticed that he'd been down that same road yesterday on his way to the Butler ranch and that was most likely what had him riled up, thinking about them.

Calling this place *convenient* was just about laughable when it would be a thirty-minute ordeal, round trip. The drive would do him good. Thinking about the past had him tense. The air was cold and he didn't like winter. It didn't help that his least favorite holiday came at the start of it. Wyatt clenched his back teeth and moved inside. He located a bottle of pain reliever and paid at the counter.

Walking out to his truck, he cursed when he saw the front flat tire. He must've picked up a nail. No surprise, given the quality of the roads and all the construction going on. Texas was booming. He was used to it living in Austin. There should be something to patch it up in his toolbox. He unlocked the door and pulled out his tool kit. Then he remembered that he'd used the last of his can of aerosol tire inflator after visiting the Brunson Falls job site two weeks ago. He'd been meaning to buy a new one.

He bent down to examine his right front tire and cursed under his breath.

"Can we help?" The voice was familiar. It sounded like the Butlers from the other day and hearing it had the same effect. It grated on his nerves.

He leaned back on his heels and turned his head to look at Dade and Dalton. They'd kept enough distance that he figured they were showing him that they weren't trying to sneak up on him and he appreciated the gesture.

"It's just a flat. I'll take care of this in no time."

"We can help put on the spare," Dalton said.

He'd taken out the spare, but he figured there'd be something he could buy in the store that would have him on his way in a few minutes. "I don't need a hand."

"You sure? We could knock that out in a minute together or give you a ride anywhere you need to go," the other one said.

"I know how to fix a flat." Wyatt was being a jerk. Seeing them reminded him of Maverick Mike Butler and the heavy thoughts he'd been having on the way over.

Everyone needed to be very clear that Wyatt could handle himself in any situation. There wasn't a case where he believed it necessary to ask someone else for help and especially not a Butler. Maybe his stubbornness came from being an only child and learning to depend on himself early in life. He'd always been the keep-to-himself type, the loner. People were under the misguided impression that a man who liked to be alone was lonely.

In Wyatt's case, the opposite couldn't be truer. He happened to like his own company. He didn't need others to validate him. And he sure as hell didn't want anything from a Butler, and that included their time.

"In case you change your mind," one of them said.

"I'm clear on what I need. I don't need your help." Wyatt had started to say *handout*. That was odd.

One of the twins bent down, set a small card next to Wyatt and placed a rock on top so it wouldn't blow away.

Wyatt glanced down. It was a business card with a cell number on it.

Hell would catch him on fire before he'd call that number.

CHANGING THE TIRE turned out to be more complicated than buying a can of aerosol and plugging up a small hole. First of all, the store was out. Figure that. With all this construction, he should've at least considered the possibility.

Waiting for another customer to show up and be willing to take him to a big-box store near the interstate took almost twenty minutes.

Fixing the tire was the easy part after he'd secured the right materials, except that it had started to drizzle and his hands nearly froze before he'd finished and was on the road again.

By the time he made it back to Meg's, his

arms were covered in dirt and he was in one hell of a fine mood.

It took a few minutes for her to answer the door, and when she did she looked like she'd been hit by a truck while he was gone. She had to squint to look at him. Movement looked to cause tremendous pain.

"What happened?" he asked out of concern.

"Headache," she responded, holding the baby. "It got worse." She hadn't seemed to be in that much pain when he'd left more than an hour ago. Now he really felt like a jerk for taking so long to get back. He reminded himself that he'd had no idea she would get this bad, but he wasn't ready to let himself off the hook. Last year, she'd canceled dinner plans more than once complaining of a headache. Even then, he'd believed she was working herself too hard. From the looks of it, she hadn't slowed down since having the baby.

They needed to have a conversation about her taking better care of herself.

Stephanie pushed past him as he followed Meg into the kitchen. Her friend glared at him as he held out the small bag.

"You're a little late, don't you think," she said, not bothering to mask her anger.

"I had a flat tire," he said.

"And, what? No spare?" she shot back.

"It's okay," Meg interrupted, her face crinkled like it hurt to speak.

Wyatt apologized again.

She looked at the bag in his hands like he was handing her a bomb. "It's fine. I don't need them anymore. Stephanie borrowed a couple from the neighbor. They'll kick in any minute. I'm already starting to feel better anyway."

This was better? Wyatt's extended hand stood between them.

She glanced at him and then the bag awkwardly. "Thanks anyway."

"You should've called," he said.

"What good would that have done with a flat tire?" Stephanie said from her spot next to the coffee machine. "Besides, I could say the same thing to you."

Wyatt wasn't used to answering to anyone else and he had to admit to being offended. There was a reason he lived in a house with one coffee mug.

And yet he still felt like the biggest jerk for not checking in.

He set the bag down on the counter beside Meg as she poured a fresh cup.

Looking at her struggling through pain was a knife stab to the chest. It would be better if he was the one suffering. That would be easier for him. Watching her, feeling helpless was the worst.

A memory broke through. He was standing beside his mother's hospital bed as she pushed the morphine-release button repeatedly, complaining of severe pain. He could see it written in the carved lines of her forehead, the pinched muscles of her face. No matter how many times she pushed that button in a row, none came. There was only so much narcotic it could dispense before it became dangerous and her pain seemed to stay above that threshold.

Meg's cell phone buzzed and she quickly answered, balancing the call and the baby. Stephanie cut across the kitchen and took the sleeping infant from Meg's arms with a disgusted look toward Wyatt. Was he supposed to know what her problem was?

He would've offered to hold the baby if it weren't for the fact that he was afraid he'd hurt the little thing. She wasn't much bigger than nothing wrapped in that tiny blanket. He'd never held something so small and so innocent in his arms.

And something with the potential to rock his world so completely.

His cell buzzed in his pocket. He fished it out and checked the screen. Dr. Raul. Based on the side of the conversation he could hear, Meg was on her phone with the sheriff. Two calls that had the potential to change Wyatt's life. The odds of both of them coming in at the same time on a normal day were ridiculously low. But this week, on *this* day any good luck he'd experienced in his life up until now could come crashing down around him.

"What did the test say?" Wyatt asked after perfunctory greetings.

The doctor hesitated before saying, "Congratulations, Mr. Jackson."

"There's no other possibility?" Wyatt wasn't sure why he asked. Part of him had known since he first put eyes on the little girl that she was his. She was an exact match to his baby picture. He expected to be disappointed by the confirmation. Confused. Hell, angry.

Strangely, he wasn't any of those things. It was as if puzzle pieces clicked together and the picture made perfect sense.

Would he have chosen this particular time

in his life to have a child? The answer was simple. No.

But she was here. She was beautiful. And he'd figure out how to move forward with an arrangement between him and Meg to make it all work.

It was most likely his practical nature and not real feelings for his child that snapped him into focus so quickly.

"These tests are never one hundred percent certain, but statistically speaking the probability that you're not the father is insignificant," the doctor answered.

"Thank you." Wyatt ended the call as Meg almost fell against the counter.

Her face was drained of color. He was grateful Stephanie was with the little one. He got to Meg's side in time to catch her, but she lost her grip on the cell she'd been holding and it crashed against the tile.

"What did he say?" Wyatt asked, ready to catch her if her legs gave out. Somewhere in the back of his mind it registered that the two of them would need to have a serious conversation about the future now that he was a father, but he drew a line around the knowledge and marked it as off-limits for now. Separating his emotions was a survival skill he'd developed as a small child out of necessity.

"The hair ribbon." Meg was trembling.

"The what?" He searched her face for something…

"It belonged to Mary Jane," she said so quietly that he almost couldn't make out the words.

"Who's that?" he asked as she started to sink toward the floor. He tightened his grip around her waist as the sound of the baby crying blasted from the room down the hall.

For a split second it dawned on him that *his* child was crying. Again he had to contain his emotions and the strangeness of the thought in order to focus on Meg.

Wyatt took most of her weight as he helped her to the kitchen chair.

"Who's Mary Jane?" he asked again.

It took a few seconds for Meg to speak, and he assumed she was gathering her courage as her gaze darted around the floor. "We were kids when she was taken. Ten years old. She was my best friend."

She looked up at him with a look of complete terror.

"He's back. He can't have my daughter," Meg

said in that determined voice of hers. "He can't take Aubrey, too."

"No one's taking my daughter." Wyatt didn't know why those words sprang out, but he wouldn't take them back if he could. This news changed things because he also realized that Meg and his daughter were being targeted. Or someone was taunting her. Could the man who had taken her friend have returned? It was a possibility too real to be discounted. Had the abductor left the ribbon on purpose? Or had the person done that to throw off investigators?

Meg gave him a look that said she knew what the doctor had told him.

"I'm guessing they never caught the guy," he said to Meg. Was this why she worked on behalf of children and women who couldn't fight for themselves? Her best friend had been abducted and the perpetrator was never brought to justice.

"We were together that day." Meg focused out the window, her gaze fixed, and she looked lost.

A shot of anger burst through him. He clenched and released his fists to stop from reaching out to touch her, to be her comfort as tears slid down her cheeks.

"What happened?"

"I don't know," she said quickly, and there was desperation in her tone. Her eyes widened and more tears fell. "I keep trying to remember. All I recall is climbing the tree. I tried to convince her to follow but she was too scared. I should've gone down to play with her but I didn't." Meg stilled. "Next thing I remember I'm in the sheriff's office being grilled about who took her. The deputy thought I knew what happened and was being insolent."

"But you didn't remember so you couldn't help," he reassured. So much made sense about why she'd chosen her line of work and then there was her tenuous relationship with the sheriff's office.

Had a monster returned? Solving a cold case that had occurred almost two decades ago might just lead Wyatt and Meg to the truth about what was going on now. But if she didn't know then what had happened, how would she remember now?

"Aubrey needs a bottle." She pushed up to her feet as the sounds of the little girl's whimpering neared.

Wyatt had no idea how to do that, but he was ready for a crash course. "Sit down until you can stand without losing your balance. Tell me what to do."

"No, it's okay—"

"The DNA test confirmed what you knew all along. Aubrey is my daughter. I owe you an apology, Meg." He softened his tone when he said, "If you'll let me, I'd like to learn how to feed her."

Meg called to her friend, who brought the baby into the room and pulled up a chair next to her. The baby wound up to cry and released a scream that shredded Wyatt's heart. He'd never heard a more gut-wrenching sound than his own daughter crying. *Daughter.* That word would take some getting used to.

"What do I need to do?"

Stephanie started toward him, but he waved her off and then washed his hands. "Give it to me one step at a time."

"The clean bottles are there on the counter. Put a packet of formula into the bottle and fill it with the distilled water from there." Meg pointed to the water purifier next to the bottles.

Wyatt did it, pleased with himself for the progress. At least there was one area in which he could contribute, maybe ease her burden.

A burst of light penetrated the wall inside his chest. "Now what?"

"It needs to be warmed. There's a warmer which I set on a timer after the last feeding. Put the bottle inside and the light will turn green when it's ready." Meg motioned toward the contraption that was smaller than a toaster.

Thirty seconds later, he was handing over the bottle to her. Thankfully, the color returned to Meg's cheeks as she looked at her daughter, *their* daughter.

The hungry baby settled as soon as she got the first drop of warm liquid in her mouth, and something that felt a lot like pride swelled in Wyatt's chest.

He didn't normally do emotion, but there was something primal and satisfying about getting this right, providing food for his child.

Wyatt was caught between a rock and a hard place. Seeing Meg look so vulnerable was chipping away at the walls he'd constructed—walls that he had no intention of bringing down except where his daughter was concerned. But there was a kicker. Could he let Aubrey in without permanently cracking the casing around his heart?

Looking down at the helpless little bug, he

knew instantly that he'd do whatever it took to protect his own, including keeping his feelings for her mother balanced. He'd been totally unprepared for the surge of attraction he felt toward Meg earlier. But that would have to stay in check.

He had to keep a clear mind in order to protect her and the daughter who'd stolen his heart from the second he'd put eyes on her. Damn. Parenting. Wyatt had never felt less prepared for any task. And a question loomed…

Could he keep all of them alive long enough to figure out who was targeting Meg and her baby…*his baby*, and why?

Chapter Eight

Holding Aubrey, hearing her baby's cries, jolted Meg away from the dark pit she'd been free-falling into. She marveled at the power the little child had over her.

Trying to remember the past took a physical toll, and she couldn't imagine doing any of this without Wyatt, either.

If she'd done one thing right in her life other than have Aubrey, it was call Wyatt when she did. He might be the added security she needed to keep her daughter safe, and Meg would make any sacrifice to put her daughter's needs first.

Was the kidnapper from her past closing in? Or did someone else know?

"The ribbon changes everything," she said to Wyatt as Aubrey drained the contents of her bottle.

"What else did the sheriff say?" he asked.

"That he would put every available deputy on the case and he'd like us to come in to discuss it," she said.

"That doesn't sound reassuring," he admitted.

"Not to me, either. There's been too much going on in this town," she said. "It used to feel safe, but not anymore. It sounded like he's rethinking his strategy in the investigation, but who knows what's really going on in his mind."

"You and the baby should come to Austin with me," he said after a thoughtful pause.

"To do what?" She couldn't see how that would help. Besides, seeing him with Aubrey made her wish for things she knew were impossible, like a real family. Watching Wyatt's protectiveness also made her realize how much her life was about to change. Their future was going to be about shared custody and spending every other Christmas with Aubrey. The thought brought tears to her eyes, but she kept them in check. Those were good problems to have in comparison to what she faced now.

"It would keep you both out of danger until we figured this out," he said. "Look, news that Butler is technically my father will break any day now if it hasn't already and that's going to bring a lot of unwanted attention to both of us. The media has been struggling to find anything worth printing, but every publication will want to be first to break the story when the sheriff finds the killer."

"Which makes going to your place seem like an even bigger mistake," she said. "Our every move will be chronicled and that could put us in a vulnerable place."

He stood up, paced. "You have a point."

"I have a couple of cases going to trial early in the new year I need to prepare—"

Wyatt was already shaking his head. "Work is going to have to take a back seat. Staying here isn't an option, either."

As much as she didn't want to admit it, he was probably right about setting her caseload aside. *For now.* Maybe Stephanie could take over for a little while until it was safe for Meg and the baby to surface. They were most likely being overly cautious, but taking unnecessary risks with Aubrey wasn't an option. Meg would have to figure out something for her cases, though. She couldn't walk away from the people depending on her any more than she could turn her back on her own child.

"Then, where do we go? What else do we

do? I wish I could remember the past. I could make all this go away for everyone's sake. Most of all, Mary Jane's parents deserved closure. I couldn't give it to them then, and I can't now. There isn't squat I can do about it even though it makes me crazy and now my daughter is in danger." Aubrey shifted position in her arms and blinked. Meg realized she was getting a little too worked up. If babies could sense emotion, she certainly didn't want her daughter to pick up on her anxiety level.

Meg took a deep breath and refocused on her daughter's face. Too many times in the past eight weeks she'd looked to that little angel when Meg doubted she'd be any good at being a mother. Her own had taken off when Meg graduated high school. Apparently, eighteen years with her was more than enough for the woman.

Shaking off that heavy thought, Meg looked up at Wyatt. He stood there, in her kitchen, his hip against her countertop, and there was something that looked so right about him being there. She took it as a good sign that maybe they'd be able to work together when it came to Aubrey. At least she prayed they could set their differences aside and figure out a way to coparent.

His arms were folded across his muscled chest, and the fabric of his shirt stretched over hard angles.

"I'm sorry that happened," he said quietly. Reverently?

"Thank you," she said.

"Someone could know that story and be trying to taunt you," he said.

"It's highly possible," she admitted. "But how would they get her hair ribbon if this person didn't take her?"

"We need to ask the sheriff," Wyatt said. "What if I take Aubrey to Austin for a while until this whole thing settles—"

Luckily, she didn't have to interrupt him. He stopped on his own.

"The determined look on your face as you hold her tells me there's no way you'd ever want to be apart from her," he supplied. "I heard what you said before but I still think my place is a good option. No one will get past security and you'd have privacy. Media aside, it's still safer than here."

"I don't hate the idea. Your town house isn't built for an infant, though," she countered.

"My house in the hills is finished. With a few adjustments, I'm sure we could make do," he said. "Whatever isn't there can be ordered. Most anything can be delivered within twenty-four hours between online shopping and lightning-fast delivery."

"I can't even think of everything she'd need," she admitted. "There's so much."

"Does that mean you're considering the idea?" His brow shot up.

"Yes. Considering, not agreeing," she clarified.

"Let's start with the basics. Where does she sleep?" he asked, and she realized that she hadn't shown him anything in the house other than the open-concept living room and kitchen. He had a lot to learn before he could be left alone with Aubrey. The thought was strangely reassuring because it would give her more time. The thought of shared custody and holidays without Aubrey was almost unbearable.

"During the day Aubrey sleeps in a bassinet in her room. At night, she stays with me. There's a crib but she's usually in bed with me," she said. The idea of getting away from Cattle Barge for a few days was growing on her. What about her caseload, though? The people who depended on her? There was no way she could let them down and his place wasn't necessarily safer, especially once the Butler news broke. "As nice as it sounds to go to your house, I was just thinking that I need to be here for work. I'm not taking on anything new, but I can't abandon the people depending on me."

"What can't be done online?" he asked.

She needed to think. Recent events, his presence and lack of sleep were clouding her judgment. She needed a good workout to clear her mind. "I can study the files and arrange services from anywhere, but I need a lot of help with the baby, and Stephanie usually takes a few feedings so I can work or take a power nap."

"When do you actually sleep?" His brow hiked.

"All the time," she countered, but just thinking about a soft pillow and warm blanket made her want to curl on her side and sleep for two days straight.

"Based on what I've seen so far, I'd have to disagree." He folded his arms across that broad chest.

"What do you think we should do next?" she

asked as she placed her—*their*—daughter over her shoulder and gently patted her back.

"I'm still trying to figure out our next move," he admitted. "I see problems with going to my place, but we definitely can't stick around here. Before this update I'd been planning to speak to Garza. See if I could get a good read on him. He seems less likely now."

Stephanie walked into the room wearing workout pants and a hoodie.

"I'm going for a run." She pulled an earbud out of her ear and checked her watch. "I'll be back in half an hour or so."

"Take your phone with you in case I need to reach you," Meg said.

Stephanie patted the front zip pouch of her hoodie. "Got it right here."

"Be careful," Meg warned. "And stay warm. It's gotten colder out there."

Her friend nodded with half a smile. "I'll be right back."

Stephanie pulled the strings to tighten the hood around her face before taking off out the back door. From the window, Meg could see her friend stretching outside. She'd replaced her earbuds and her head was slightly bobbing to the music.

"Do you have family nearby?" Wyatt asked, and she realized how little she'd shared with him even though they'd dated for several months last year while she spent weeks at a time meeting with lawmakers in the capital. She knew surprisingly little about him, as well.

"I never knew my dad," she admitted. "Mom took off after I graduated. Afraid it's just me and Aubrey. That little girl is all the family I have aside from Stephanie, who is more like a sister than a friend. What about you? What's going on with your family?"

"You already know who my biological father was." He raked a hand through his bronzed curls. "Mom passed away five years ago."

"Then we're in the same boat as far as parents go," she said. "The main difference is that you have brothers and sisters."

"No, I don't." An emotion flashed in his eyes that gave her a shock. "I have a daughter and that's the only family I lay claim to."

"Didn't you have a meeting with the Butlers the other day? What happened?" she asked.

"Nothing I wanted to hear."

"It's fine if you don't want me to know," she said a little more briskly than she'd intended. If they were going to coparent it was reasonable to learn about each other's family history. The pediatrician had already asked questions about Aubrey's father's side of the family that Meg couldn't answer.

"Believe me, there's nothing to tell." The bull in Wyatt came out in full force. The man had a stubborn streak.

A shrill scream pierced the air.

"Stephanie." Meg stood and bolted for the door.

"You stay here and lock the door behind me," Wyatt warned, blocking her exit until she nodded agreement.

Meg did as he suggested. The baby stirred. The sudden movement must've startled her awake, but Meg was grateful her daughter was in her arms. Any hope yesterday's attack could've been random shot out the window. She scrambled to the front room and looked outside, wishing she could see something.

Pulse racing, Meg scanned the area looking for someone, something, some kind of threat. But there was nothing and her worst fears came into play. Had Stephanie been abducted?

Meg forced back the tears threatening. A sob escaped anyway. Her body shook with fear.

Nothing could happen to her friend.

For a split second, Meg wondered if the attacks were meant for Stephanie, but that wouldn't make any sense given the ribbon. And then she really thought about it. It was her best friend who had been abducted all those years ago. And now her current best friend had been targeted. Maybe, as odd as it sounded even to her, the person behind these attacks was trying to make Meg pay by hurting those closest to her.

It was a farfetched theory, but that's what she could come up with while this tired, even with adrenaline pumping through her body.

Aubrey belted out a cry and made a face so pitiful that Meg's heart squeezed.

"It's okay, sweet girl," she soothed before feeling her daughter's forehead. Aubrey wasn't warm and that was reassuring. She'd caught a cold at two weeks old and that had nearly scared Meg to death. Everything had turned out to be fine, except for Meg's nerves. She feared they would never recover, and after the events of the past twenty-four hours hope dwindled further.

Meg gently bounced up and down and that seemed to soothe the baby enough for her to close her eyes again. There was no sign of

Wyatt or Stephanie, and that fact sent cold chills racing up her spine. *Please be okay. Both of you.*

Minutes ticked by with nothing, causing Meg's pulse to spike with every tick toward the new hour. And then she saw them. Stephanie was being carried by Wyatt, who was almost in a dead run.

As soon as he hopped onto the porch, Meg opened the door. The blast of cold entered before they did, and Meg shivered. Seeing Stephanie sent Meg's heart into a free fall. Her lip was busted and her cheeks were red from blunt force.

"Lock the door and call 911," Wyatt said before setting Stephanie down on the couch.

"Is she—" Meg put Aubrey in the swing, started it so the baby would stay comforted and then palmed her cell. She punched in the three digits reserved for emergencies and listened as the line rang.

"Unconscious," he said, and she noticed for the first time there was a lot of blood covering his hand. He moved swiftly as he went to work, locating supplies like clean towels and wet wipes. "The person who did this to her ran away when he saw me coming. He just dropped her and she went limp like a rag doll. I started to go after him, but he was too far and she was in bad shape. Plus, I didn't want to take the chance he could somehow get to you and the baby before I got back. I don't know this area well enough, so I picked her up and brought her home."

Meg relayed the information to the operator, requesting an ambulance and the sheriff. When the call ended, she ran to Stephanie's side. "What can I do?"

Wyatt scanned the door and then the windows. "Make sure all the doors and windows are locked and that no one enters who isn't wearing a badge or looks like an EMT."

"I couldn't tell if her chest was moving or not. Is she breathing?" Meg asked as she double-checked the locks.

"Yes." He pressed a clean white towel to her skull. A few seconds later, he pulled it back and the white had transformed to red. He replaced the cloth with a fresh one immediately.

Meg moved to his side and took the soaked rag.

"She has a cut above her forehead and foreheads are bleeders." He cleared a little of the area and the cut immediately bled. "It probably looks worse than it is."

Stephanie blinked her eyes open and mumbled something unintelligible. She needed to stay away from Meg if she wanted to be safe from now on. Meg would figure out a way to make that happen. She would do whatever was necessary in order to keep her friend out of danger.

Memories assaulted Meg. Her brain hurt and all she could see was fog.

"He called me Meg," Stephanie said, trying to blink her eyes open. "He thought I was you."

Meg gasped. "I'm so sorry this happened."

Wyatt shot a look meant to be reassuring. Nothing could console Meg. She was toxic to everyone she cared about.

"Did you see who did this to you?" Wyatt asked Stephanie.

The sound of glass breaking in the kitchen caused Meg to jump.

"Stay with her," Wyatt instructed with a narrowed gaze.

Meg was already by Stephanie's side, holding her hand. The noise must've roused Aubrey because she started winding up to cry.

"Go," Stephanie said, and it sounded like it took a lot of effort.

"I'll be right back," Meg said, feeling torn between caring for the immediate medical needs of her friend and attending to her baby who was startled but otherwise fine.

Sirens burst through the chaos. Clearly the emergency or law-enforcement vehicle was still at a distance, but the sound was wailing closer. She could only pray the noise would run off whoever had broken the window. The world felt like it had collapsed around her in the past half hour.

"Help is coming," she said to Stephanie, who was already trying to sit up. "Stay put until someone can take a look at your head."

Stephanie tried to roll over to her side. "I might be sick."

"She's not well," Meg shouted to Wyatt. She couldn't leave her friend's side, not while she was in this bad a shape and trying to get up.

The sirens were getting closer and she realized an ambulance was almost there.

Wyatt bolted into the room. "If there's someone out there, I didn't see him."

"What was the noise?" Meg asked.

"A rock was tossed through the kitchen window. I'm guessing the sirens scared him away," he supplied, dropping down at Stephanie's side. "Stay right here. You're going to be fine."

With Wyatt there to care for Stephanie, Meg discarded the bloody towel and used baby wipes to clean her hands. She picked up the baby, who was trying to suck on her fingers, and located a pacifier. Aubrey calmed down almost instantly.

"He confused the two of us," Meg said to him as she rocked the baby across her shoulder. Between the sirens, the stress and her child's crying, Meg was one step away from losing it. She took a few calming breaths.

"From the back, I can see where he might," Wyatt said. Frustration and stress creased his forehead.

No one was safe near Meg anymore.

"We have to split up, Wyatt."

Chapter Nine

Wyatt stared at Meg, who looked to be standing guard at the door to Stephanie's room in the ER. Wyatt had played enough football in his youth to know that a blow to the head needed to be taken seriously. Stephanie was resting peacefully for now. A deputy had taken her statement during the brief time she was awake. The doctor had been optimistic for a full recovery as long as Stephanie took it easy for a few weeks.

He contemplated Meg's earlier comment about splitting up. There was no way he could let her or his daughter out of his sight without going insane. But the time for the conversation was not now. Stephanie's well-being was top priority.

Meg paced another lap around the room.

"They're keeping her overnight for observation, but where will she go when she's released? I don't want her going home alone and she moved in with me six months ago when she left her boyfriend." Meg's voice wasn't much more than a whisper, but he picked up on the seriousness. Of course, she would want to take care of her friend. Stephanie was in trouble because of her association with Meg. Given her past, Meg would take that to heart.

Besides, she made a good point. Stephanie had been a good friend to Meg during her pregnancy and these early weeks with the baby. He wanted to do something to help her out.

It was easy to see that Meg bore the burden of guilt, blaming herself for everything that was going on. He didn't want her to feel that way. He wanted to somehow ease her stress, telling himself that it wasn't because he cared about Meg but that it wasn't good for the baby.

"What about your contacts? Part of your job is to place people in care while they sort out their lives," he said.

Meg's eyes lit up. "Of course. I know the perfect person to call." She glanced down at the sleeping baby in her arms and then back to him. "Could you hold her for a minute?"

Wyatt took the baby in his arms, worrying he

would crush the little thing. "She can't weigh more than ten pounds."

"She's twelve-point-five pounds according to her doctor last week," Meg clarified.

"That seems small," he said, although he had no idea how much a baby was supposed to weigh.

"She's right on target and pretty average for her age actually." Meg sounded a little put off. Hell, he wasn't trying to offend her. Aubrey was the tiniest thing he'd ever held. Under different circumstances, he might find Meg's defensiveness sweet and a little bit funny. Sexy, too. Right now, all he could focus on was keeping her and the baby safe while making arrangements for Stephanie.

"If you think she's so light, try carrying her around for two hours straight. Your arms burn and they feel like they're going to break off," Meg added.

"You're good with her," he said by way of apology.

"I've had eight weeks of practice," Meg conceded as she dug around in her purse for her cell. She located it and started toward the hallway.

"If you don't mind, I'd like you to stay where

I can keep you in full view," he said, not wanting to cause undue stress but at the same time realizing it was difficult to manage holding a baby and still be ready should someone sneak past security and come at Meg. However unlikely the scenario might be, Wyatt wasn't taking any chances.

Meg nodded with a somber expression and he knew she understood fully the reason he'd asked. Even with hospital security on alert, someone could sneak in. It was a big place. If not the attacker, then media could slip past the front desk and the guard at the nurse's station. Bringing attention to anyone connected to Meg or the baby right now wasn't advisable.

He glanced down at the little bundle in his arms. She was secured in a tight blanket, sleeping peacefully. Another burst of pride filled his chest. How could something so tiny break down his carefully constructed walls so easily? He still had no idea what the future held, but he knew this little girl would play a large part in it.

Meg smiled for the first time today, and there was something satisfying about being the one to put it there. "We've done a lot of work with a women's shelter. Ava Becks is the director. She's good at keeping people out of sight and under the radar while keeping some sense of a normal life for them. She's set up this entire compound where women can do things like shop for food, clothing and get a haircut without ever leaving the safety of the complex. Maybe Stephanie can hide out there until everything blows over. She'd be able to work remotely in order to keep her cases going and keep a schedule. She can go for a jog without being afraid someone will attack her."

The place sounded like the promised land for battered women. While Wyatt hated there was a need for such a facility, he appreciated what was being done. His fists nearly balled thinking about the reason innocent women and children would need such a place. When this was all over, he'd look into setting up an annual donation. His general manager, Marcus Field, had mentioned the employees would like to join together for a volunteer day around the holidays. He'd put Ava's shelter on the list. With twenty-five profitable locations of his restaurant across southwest Texas, he could do a lot of good for the charity and he'd do it in Aubrey's name. Which also gave him another idea. This one he didn't like as much...

"You and the baby could join her," Wyatt

offered, taking a hit to the chest at the suggestion even though it was his suggestion. "I'd like to come, too. I know you mentioned splitting up earlier but I'd rather not. Now that I know about her I'd be crazy with worry if I couldn't see that she was safe."

Meg was already shaking her head. "Now that I think about I've changed my mind. It's too risky. I don't want to bring any unnecessary attention to Ava's operation. I could jeopardize her entire staff, not to mention her tenants, who rely on the place being off the radar. Ava's amazing at what she does for people, believe me, and I want my situation to be as far away from her and her people as possible." Meg looked at Stephanie. "And her. She's been lucky twice. If anything happened to…"

Emotion seemed to get the best of her. She turned her back and sniffed.

"Nothing will. She'll be tucked away on one of my properties, out of sight and kept safe." He wanted to tell her how strong she was for making that decision. She was right, too. In a weak moment, he'd considered making a call to the Butlers to see what they could offer. But how would that help? There was a swarm of media on their doorstep and Mike Butler's killer still hadn't been found. For all Wyatt knew he was right under their noses and no one in the family had figured it out. Not exactly his idea of a safe place for Stephanie, Aubrey or Meg.

"As soon as Stephanie wakes, we'll fill her in on the plan," Meg said, her smile still in place. It didn't reach her eyes, but it was a start.

He glanced down at his daughter. The thought of Aubrey being his only living family hit harder than he expected. Maybe knowing he was a father now was softening him. He wished his mother was alive to meet his little girl. The expansion of his restaurant chain had consumed him and, if he was being honest, gave him a good reason to set aside his grief.

He'd seen to it that his mother had had a proper funeral that year and then he'd buried all his emotions with her. He'd become a workhorse, a machine that never needed sleep.

For the first time in his life, he felt tired.

"I CAN MAKE COFFEE," Meg offered after feeding the baby again.

Checking into an all-suite hotel should keep them under the radar for the time being. The one-bedroom was well-appointed and had all the basics, including a nice-sized bathroom and generous living/kitchen area with a full-size fridge and microwave.

"Don't get up," he said, noticing the dark circles cradling her eyes. He needed to keep his distance because he kept thinking about the kiss they'd shared. It hadn't felt like a mistake at the time. Now, he realized it had felt a little too right.

"I need to set her down for a little while before my arms fall off," Meg said. They'd requested a crib and within ten minutes of their arrival one of the maintenance men had arrived to set it up next to the bed, for more convenient nighttime feedings.

Seeing how caring for an infant was a round-the-clock necessity made him tired thinking about it. He could be honest with himself. He had no idea how Meg was doing it. She took care of a baby who fed every two hours. The feedings lasted for almost a half hour and then she was right back at it an hour-and-a-half later. On top of that, she was co-running a successful organization.

He'd only found out he was a father a few hours ago and he was already tired from worry—worry that had been foreign to him until he found out that Aubrey was his child.

Then worry had heaped on top of him, covering his arms like cement.

Wyatt's relationship with the little girl's mother was a work in progress, a challenging one at that given his back-and-forth feelings, but they had time to figure things out, right?

Not if a maniac gets his way, Wyatt thought.

Meg crossed her arms and leaned against the counter. He caught her studying him.

"Ready to go to the sheriff's office?" he asked. He'd told Sawmill that they'd stop by to give statements.

"I can't believe my house is a crime scene," Meg admitted with a yawn. "I don't want to disturb the baby yet."

Looking at her while she stood there, Wyatt could see that his feelings weren't the only issue. Her body language said she was closed off. Given her history, he doubted if she'd ever truly let another person in other than their daughter. Meg was on guard at all times and it finally dawned on him that was the emotion he'd picked up on last year. He'd never met a woman with walls constructed higher than his own and chalked both up to crazy childhoods.

"Tell me the truth. How long has it been since you've slept?" he asked.

"Me? I'm fine," she responded, biting back another yawn.

"Close your eyes and try to get some rest." He had no intention of letting Meg or his daughter out of his sight and he could stay awake as long as he needed to.

"Every time I close my eyes I think about her, about my friend. The recent attempt on Aubrey and the sheriff finding the ribbon seemed to be bringing up painful memories from the past." Meg looked at him with an expression that stirred something deep in his chest.

"Will it help to talk about it?" he asked.

"Can't hurt," she said. "I can't help but wonder what kind of monster would take a child. For eighteen years I haven't forgotten he existed. I'd hoped he was dead. I'd see Mary Jane's family in the store not long after it happened. She has a brother two years older than me. I never knew what to say to him. He tried to talk to me a few weeks after Aubrey was born. He seemed upset. He kept looking at Aubrey and then me." She paused. "After all these years I still couldn't face him. I ran out of the store so fast there was no way he could catch up to me. My cart was there by the checkout.

I'd spent half an hour in the store before abandoning everything but my daughter."

"What happened when you were young wasn't your fault." He'd read the article she'd pulled up from over the summer. Every tidbit of news had been drudged up from the past it seemed ever since Maverick Mike was killed, including Mary Jane's kidnapping and death. "And neither is any of this. You didn't do this to her family. This happened to you, too. Both of you were little kids at the time."

"That may be true, but I sure didn't offer much help to find her. I must've seen his face. I was right there." She stared at him. "Why can't I remember? How hard would that be? Maybe law enforcement could've gotten to her in time, rescued her before he killed her and she disappeared forever."

"You were a child. Didn't you say that you were ten-years-old? Again, I don't think you should blame yourself because law enforcement—who were grown men and women, by the way—didn't do the job they were supposed to," he countered. And then a thought struck. What if someone had figured out that Aubrey was his child? What if that person was trying to kidnap her with the intention of getting ransom money? "Do you think there's any possibility the attempt on Aubrey could be related to the fact that she's a Butler? If that's true these cases wouldn't be linked."

"They have to be. Where else would her hair ribbon come from? What are the chances it would be at the attempted kidnapping scene of my daughter?" She had a point. He was trying to offer other explanations.

"It's possible the ribbon was stolen from an evidence room," he said, trying to throw out other options. "Someone could be trying to rattle you or throw you and the sheriff off. Hell, they could be trying to shake up local law enforcement."

"Let's just say that's possible. Who would benefit from doing that?" she asked.

"You work as a family advocate in abuse cases. We need to look harder at the fathers and dig deeper into your cases. It's still possible this could be motivated by revenge and has nothing to do with what happened when you were a child. Someone could be trying to manipulate your feelings. Throw you off balance."

Her eyes widened. "I guess I didn't even think about that."

It looked like her mind was clicking through possibilities.

"Based on what I've heard so far of your work, the list of people not thrilled with your operation is long."

"Are you blaming me for this? Saying I somehow deserve it?" Her lips thinned.

"Hold on. I didn't say anything like that," he defended. "We need to examine all angles, and sometimes the obvious one is the right one."

She looked exacerbated and he couldn't figure out…

Hold on.

Did she think he was trying to dig up dirt so he could fight her for custody? The way she'd bucked up for a fight had him going down that path.

"I've worked on a few cases in the past year. There are always threats in the early stages, and blame and anger. It's usually directed at me in the beginning." She sighed sharply.

"Let's look at the most recent and we can work our way back from there," he said, and he was relieved when his suggestion seemed to calm her rattled nerves a little bit more. If he could do that more often, it would be good for their little girl. Those last three words still sounded foreign.

Wyatt needed to get used to the idea he had a daughter. Granted, Meg had had nearly a year to prepare herself for this day, and all this had been thrust on him in the past twenty-four hours, less if he counted since he'd received confirmation.

He'd risen to meet bigger challenges.

Patience and logic were all he needed to overcome any obstacle.

And that's what he needed to do now. Take a step back. Evaluate the situation. Come up with a plan of attack.

He glanced at the screen of his phone. "If my calculations are correct, the little bug in the next room is going to need to eat again in approximately forty-five minutes."

"That seems to be all she does right now," Meg said. She added quickly, "The doctor said it's perfectly normal. She's perfectly healthy."

Meg wrung her hands together.

"We don't have a lot of time before she needs attention and I'd rather not discuss the case when she's awake," he said.

"Or in the room at all," Meg added.

"Agreed." They'd just made their first decree as parents. It wasn't as difficult as Wyatt thought it might be. Meg was an intelligent and reasonable woman. Her mind was the first thing he'd been attracted to. Okay, fine, it was her eyes. But he'd noticed her intelligence the minute she spoke. They'd talked music—she loved a good old bluegrass melody—and current events.

And she knew how to cook. Not that he was a sexist jerk or bought any of that nonsense about women belonging in the kitchen. But there wasn't anything much sexier than a beautiful woman who was confident in the kitchen and actually enjoyed the process of creating a meal.

He glanced at the counter, remembering the pasta machine she'd brought to his place on their second date. She'd rolled out dough from scratch. She'd flattened it and fed it into the machine, catching the long strands of fettuccini noodles as they came out the other end. The look on her face, the enjoyment at creating something that she knew would taste better than anything he'd ever seen on a plate. And he was no slouch. But his culinary skills were limited to meats on the grill—which were his specialty—and ended with the perfect taco, around which he'd built his entire fortune.

He thought about the expansion. The problems. The lake house that seemed out of reach.

His work headaches were racking up, but they paled in comparison to the thought of anything happening to his child. Strange, he'd only been a parent for a few hours and his priorities were already shifting.

He wanted to get his bearings as a father. It wouldn't do any good to demand rights when he had no experience caring for an infant. He didn't even have friends with kids.

Hell, when he really thought about it he didn't have any close friends, either. He'd had a few beers with a few of his managers from time to time, called it a meeting. Wyatt had thrown everything he had, including all his time and energy, into making his chain a success. Looking back, he'd always been somewhat of a loner.

Somewhat?

He almost chuckled out loud. He'd preferred his own company to most of the young guys in high school. He never could relate considering he'd had a job since he was old enough to string together enough odd jobs to help out his mother with a few of their bills.

And speaking of money. He'd jumped the gun when he'd accused Meg of wanting to get a hold of Butler money the other day. Her reaction had seemed genuine. He'd hurt her feelings without meaning to. It had been a knee-jerk reaction and he regretted it.

Moving forward, he'd keep a better handle on what he said.

He needed to apologize for being a jerk. "I've been way off base and an apology doesn't begin to cover it, but it's a good place to start. I'm sorry, Meg. I've been acting like a real pain when I should've been supportive. I could make excuses, blame my past, but that doesn't cut it."

"We're both working through some intense emotions," she said. "I think we know better than to go down that road again. Kissing was a mistake."

Confusion struck him. She'd changed gears on him so fast he hadn't had time to hit the clutch.

Because that kiss was the first thing that had felt right to Wyatt in a long time. It was a dangerous sentiment considering he and Meg would have to figure out how to care for a child and stay on good terms.

Leading with his emotions would be a bullet through his chest when she pushed him away again. And she would.

For that little girl's sake, he wouldn't allow that to happen. No matter how much he wanted to haul Meg against his chest and kiss her again.

Chapter Ten

Aubrey was fed and burped. Wyatt had just arrived at Meg's house in order to drive the three of them to the sheriff's office.

The little girl made a face—*the* face—and Meg frowned. "She's going to need a diaper change."

"I'll take care of it." Wyatt looked a little uncertain.

"It's no problem. It'll take me two seconds," she said, holding on to Aubrey a little defensively.

"I have to learn to do it sooner or later," he countered, holding his arms out awkwardly.

Meg took a fortifying breath. He was right about one thing. He needed to learn how to take care of Aubrey, and diaper changing was a big part of the deal. At least she could stand over his shoulder and guide him through the process.

Reluctantly, she handed over Aubrey and Meg half expected her little angel to cry. Her doctor had said something about babies being sensitive to their environments and able to pick up on the emotions of others. For as awkward as Wyatt looked holding their daughter, he must be steady as steel on the inside because Aubrey didn't so much as flinch during the exchange. Of course, she was busy doing something else. The product of which wrinkled Meg's nose. *Okay, buddy. Here goes full-force fatherhood.*

"Diapers are in her bag and—"

Wyatt waved her off.

"Don't you think you should let me help you?"

"I can figure it out," he said dismissively before disappearing into the next room.

Meg wanted to chase after him and tell him that he'd been a father all of twenty-four hours and that diaper changing wasn't easy with a squirmy baby. Plus, as soon as that diaper came off Aubrey had a tendency to finish her business. She stopped herself. He wanted to do this on his own. So be it. Far be it from her to stop him.

Impatient, she tapped her toe on the carpeting while standing by the door. What was taking so long?

Meg knew better than to poke the bear and especially while he was handling their daughter. Plus, she really didn't want Aubrey to pick up on the tension between her parents. *Parents?* The word still seemed like Meg was talking about someone else and not her and Wyatt.

The proof was in the other room, most likely giving her father a hard time.

Under different circumstances, it might be funny. But then if she and Wyatt had met again without a baby in the picture she was pretty certain a whole lot of other things would be occurring in the bedroom instead of diaper changing. Things that had started her down a bad path a year ago.

For Aubrey's sake, Meg needed to find middle ground with Wyatt. The thought of someone else being in her daughter's life was a little jarring. Did he deserve to know his daughter? No question. Did Aubrey have a right to know her father? Absolutely. It was the shared custody, the part about spending every other Christmas away from her little girl that broke Meg's heart. She had never envisioned having a family like this. But, then, Aubrey hadn't been exactly planned. And Meg had never seen herself as the house, minivan and two-point-five-kids type.

She glanced at her watch. If this diaper changing process dragged on much longer it would be time for Aubrey to feed again. "Everything okay in there?"

"Of course," came the slightly too-urgent response. It was the sound of someone who was most likely drowning trying to play it cool.

Okay, Wyatt. Let's see what happens.

Wyatt reemerged, almost immediately handing Aubrey over. He looked like he'd just been through a CrossFit class at the gym as he raked his hand through his hair—the sure sign he wasn't as in control as he pretended to be.

A small part of Meg was relieved because those first few weeks with her little angel had been hard. Getting the hang of diapering and every other duty that came with the role wasn't exactly second nature to Meg. She'd grown up alone, without younger siblings or cousins to learn the ropes with. The nurses had had to teach her all the basics before leaving the hospital and she'd watched what felt like a hundred videos on the internet for reference. Then there were the mommy blogs she frequented. Becoming a mother felt like showing up to a job interview in her underwear. But, a few weeks in, Meg had started to get the hang of things. It was amazing what twenty-four-hours-a-day on-the-job training did to bring a person up to speed.

Meg cradled her daughter and stared at the sweet face cooing up at her. Her stress levels calmed enough for her to say to Wyatt, "Ready?"

She didn't want to look at the diaper because it was pretty haphazard and she could only imagine what waited underneath that blanket. Besides, he'd get the hang of it in time, and the look on his face was priceless, no matter how much he tried to cover. He was stressed. Under any other circumstance, they'd be laughing right now. Maybe even enjoying the fact they'd brought this little miracle into the world.

But the circumstances they faced were far from funny.

WYATT PUT HIS considerable size between the members of the media and Meg and the baby as soon as the trio arrived at the sheriff's office. He knew full well the extra attention wasn't going to help matters for them. His high profile could place Meg and the baby in worse jeopardy, but walking away and leaving them to fend for themselves wasn't an option.

Thinking of Aubrey, another pang of regret filled him that his mother wasn't around to meet her granddaughter. When his child had looked up at him and smiled out of the right side of her mouth, it was his mother's smile. Renee Jackson's life had been tough. She'd done the best she could. If Wyatt's no-account father had been around or had sent even a little support her life would've been so much better. Since Wyatt wasn't the lick-his-wounds type, he was grateful that he'd been shown the bad side of humanity. It had caused him to learn early on that he was the only person who could dig himself out of his own circumstances.

And he'd done pretty well for himself.

The sheriff looked as tired and overworked as the last time Wyatt had seen the man.

"Thank you for coming in," Sawmill said. "Please, make yourself comfortable."

Instead of pointing toward the chairs opposite his desk, he motioned toward the sofa on the other side of the room.

The little girl in Meg's arms started balling

her fists and punching some unseen object in the air. She looked like she was about to cry and Meg seemed distressed. She checked her bottom and then pulled her hand from the baby's bottom, soaked.

Meg stood and her blouse was wet, too. To make matters worse, the diaper practically fell off.

Now the baby was crying. Her mother was shaken. And Wyatt only had himself to blame. Diapering his daughter turned out to be trickier than he'd expected, and his damn pride had kept him from asking for help. He'd wanted to show her he could figure it out for himself and instead had made a literal mess of things. Damn.

Wyatt could see that he was going to have to make some changes if he wanted to coparent the right way. He apologized to Meg. He would've been frustrated if the shoe were on the other foot. It was a good lesson in humility. He was starting to see that he didn't have to take everything on alone when it came to Aubrey.

Ten minutes later, the baby was dry and secured in her mother's arms sucking on her fingers. Meg looked natural holding a baby.

Or maybe that primal part of him thought she looked natural holding *his* baby.

Once everyone was settled again, the sheriff continued, "Can I get you a drink? Coffee? Water?"

"No, thanks," Meg said.

Sawmill folded his hands and leaned forward, resting his elbows on his knees. "Forensics was able to pick up a DNA sample from the hair ribbon."

Meg gasped and her face paled. "And?"

"I have a name. Clayton Glass." The sheriff paused before showing a photo.

It looked as though Meg was searching her memory for recognition. Seconds stretched on as she seemed to come up empty. She shrugged with a helpless-sounding sigh.

"I shouldn't be surprised you don't recognize him," Sawmill conceded. "He isn't from around here. He said that he happened to be driving through the city that afternoon eighteen years ago when he saw the two of you. He denied having any previous interaction with either of you prior to that day and it seems as though we can take him on his word."

Tears streamed down Meg's cheeks as looked at the photo of the man who'd taken her friend's life and devastated so many others. Wyatt took the baby from her and when Meg made eye contact, a fireball swirled in his chest. Intense emotion churned behind those blue eyes of hers. An urgent need to protect her, to take away her pain, ripped through his chest. His muscles pulled taut and hot anger licked through his veins.

The baby cooed and he had to force a sense of calm even though what he really wanted to do was show Clayton Glass what it was like to take on someone his own size instead of preying on innocent children. The damage he'd done to Mary Jane's family was irrevocable. As a new father holding an innocent little girl in his arms, Wyatt's heart clenched thinking about what had happened.

"Did he say what he did to her?" Meg asked, and Wyatt picked up on the devastation in her voice.

The sheriff bowed his head as though steeling his resolve. "According to his confession, she's been gone for quite some time."

"I could've stopped him," she said through a sob.

"No, you couldn't have." The sheriff didn't miss a beat. "He confessed to watching and waiting for you to climb the tree. He baited Mary Jane to get her across the street without alerting you. You were reading a book and seemed absorbed by it. In the interview, he bragged about being able to slip her out from underneath everyone's noses."

"If I'd been paying attention," she continued, unwilling or unable to accept that she wasn't at fault, "she would still be here."

"He saw an opportunity and took it," Sawmill said, his voice even. "That wasn't anyone else's fault but Glass's. He's evil through and through. And he'll never see the light of day again."

"So, you have him in custody?" Meg's apprehension mirrored Wyatt's own. "It's over?"

"We do." Sawmill nodded. "And we have had for some time."

"Meaning?" Meg pressed.

"He's been in lockup at Huntsville prison for a little more than ten years. I'm sorry," Sawmill said with sincerity.

"What about the ribbon? How'd that turn up the other day?" she asked.

"We lost evidence to several cold cases last year. One of my deputies believed the boxes had been marked wrong and were destroyed," Sawmill admitted.

"I need a minute," Meg said, looking as though she was fighting a breakdown.

"Take all the time you need," Wyatt said.

She excused herself and disappeared down the hall toward the restroom.

It took a full fifteen minutes for her to return, and Wyatt's heart squeezed when he saw her red-rimmed eyes. The boogeyman who'd haunted her for most of her life had a name. The truth was out. Wyatt could only imagine what that might feel like.

Meg reclaimed her seat but kept her head down.

"Are you okay to move forward?" the sheriff asked, after offering more sympathy. "We can do this another time."

"Enough time has passed and I need to know who's after my little girl if not him." She'd pulled the baby's burping cloth from her diaper bag and held on to it so tightly her knuckles were white.

"Has anyone from the Fjord family reached out to you in the past six months?" he asked.

"Me? No. Not officially. I bumped into Jonathon at the grocery store over the summer, but we didn't speak. Besides, I'm pretty sure that I'm the last person anyone in that family wants to see, let alone talk to," Meg admitted. She seemed caught off guard by the suggestion. "Why?"

"I spoke to Mrs. Fjord," he supplied. "I'd like to speak to the entire family again more in depth. Time can sometimes offer perspective, and there might've been something missed on the initial round of investigations."

"Like what? You have a name. What more could you want?" she asked.

"He might've been working with a partner. Someone who is still out there," he said.

Wyatt noticed the sheriff didn't mention that would be the person trying to taunt Meg now. But what would be the motive?

"If not for Mary Jane's crime, why is Glass in prison?" Meg's voice shook but she seemed determined to finish the interview.

"He had a laundry list of charges. The biggest was armed robbery, and that's what he's currently serving time for," he supplied.

Wyatt glanced from Meg to the sheriff. "If the guy responsible for murdering Mary Jane is in prison, then who had access to the evidence room?"

"We're checking into the logs from around that time as we speak, which, unfortunately, takes us back to square one with this investigation." Sawmill looked at Meg. "I'd like a list of acquaintances and anyone you've had a disagreement with recently. It could be a coworker or client. If anyone so much as cut you off in traffic and you have a name I want it."

"As far as coworkers go, you already know Stephanie. We have a receptionist, Amy Sharp. I can write down her contact information for you," she started.

"Does she have any reason to have a grievance with you?" he asked.

"No." Meg rocked back and forth a little faster as the questions continued, and he could tell that she was getting worked up. She was working the cloth in her hands pretty hard.

"Did you check into the name she already gave?" Wyatt asked, referring to the Garza case.

"He was coaching a team in a holiday tournament in Houston at the time of the attempted abduction. There are twenty witnesses," the sheriff supplied. "We broke up the list and each person was contacted by one of my deputies."

Wyatt appreciated the thoroughness.

Under the circumstances, he couldn't blame Meg for being unsettled. He wanted to be there for her and shield the baby, which seemed an impossible task. Since he wasn't capable of caring for the eight-week-old on his own, he resigned himself to the fact she'd have to go everywhere with them.

The sheriff turned to Wyatt. "How are you connected to this case?"

Wyatt glanced at Meg, who seemed to catch on because she nodded slightly, and he took that as permission to keep talking. "I'm Aubrey's father."

Sawmill's eyebrow arched. "How many people knew you were a Butler before you came to town?"

"Only the Butlers and their lawyer as far as I know," Wyatt admitted.

An emotion flickered behind the sheriff's eyes that took a second to discern. He remembered the articles about Cadence Butler trying to run Madelyn Kensington off when she'd first come to Cattle Barge. Cadence had pulled a stunt to try to scare the former reporter so she'd leave town and the Butler family—along with her inheritance—alone.

"You think one of them would get involved with something like this? To what end?" Wyatt asked.

The sheriff's gaze bounced from Wyatt to Meg, but to his credit he didn't comment. Wyatt didn't care if the man was in law enforcement, if he made Meg uncomfortable over their situation the two of them would have words. His and Meg's relationship might be complicated, but judgment was off-limits to outsiders.

"As to your question about who knew Maverick Mike was my sperm donor, you're asking the wrong person." The sheriff needed to talk to the people at the ranch. "My last name is and always will be Jackson."

"I'll have Janis check news outlets and see when they started reporting, so we can get an idea of the scope," Sawmill said.

Meg made a noise. "News about you, us, is out?"

The sheriff nodded.

"That complicates things, doesn't it?" she asked Sawmill.

"It could," he admitted. "We'll focus on those closest to you first. Without any evidence other than the hair ribbon, we have nothing else to tie the killer in. It could be a sick prank or someone trying to get revenge."

"You asked if I had any contact with her family before," she continued. "Her parents haven't spoken to me since…"

"We're in the process of tracking her brother, Jonathon, down now," Sawmill said. "His mother said he moved out of town for his work as a bricklayer."

Wyatt couldn't imagine the pain Mary Jane's family had gone through losing their little girl so young. Looking at his own daughter, his protective instincts flared at the thought of anything happening to her. Now that he knew what Meg had been through he wondered if that's what had made her pull back from him when things started getting interesting between them. He didn't do long-term, but he'd liked spending time with her, and his current attraction most likely was crackling embers from the flame that had burned brightly a year ago.

Watching her recover after his mess-up with the diaper made him want to work together with her. It also made him feel like a jerk for not accepting help when she'd offered. He'd been so intent on figuring everything out for himself that he'd made everything worse. Wyatt wasn't used to depending on anyone else. It made him feel…helpless…and reminded him of how awful he'd felt when he couldn't do anything to ease his mother's pain before her death.

Being stubborn had made him the success he was in business…

Speaking of work, his phone hadn't stopped buzzing inside his pocket since they'd walked into the sheriff's office. That didn't signal good news. The longer this day wore on the worse it got.

And just when he thought the crap-day limit had been hit, Dade Butler knocked on the sheriff's door.

"Can I come in?" the Butler twin asked with a nod toward Sawmill.

Sheriff Sawmill stood. "My apologies in advance, but Mr. Butler asked me to let him know when you came in. He said he has an offer for both of you and that you need to hear him out."

Meg shot a confused look at Wyatt.

"There's nothing for us to hear," he said.

"Can I speak to my half-brother alone?" Dade asked the sheriff.

Sawmill excused himself.

Wyatt stood between Meg and Dade, shielding her and the baby from what he wasn't exactly sure.

"I'm here to offer any assistance you need," Dade said with a sincere look.

"You were sent?" Wyatt arched his brow.

"I volunteered, but that's not the point." Dade folded his arms. "The way I see it, you can use a hand."

"I'm afraid you'll have to fill me in," Wyatt said, unmoved. He had no idea what kind of game the Butlers were playing, but he had enough on his plate without adding them as complications. "What help have you decided we need?"

"All the media attention surrounding our father's murder has brought out a lot of crazies. Several of our family members have already been targets and we've been fortunate so far that no one has been hurt," Dade said with that same look of sincerity.

"My daughter isn't a Butler," Wyatt countered. "And neither am I."

"That may well be in your eyes, but not everyone might see it that way," Dade said. "I read someone attempted to kidnap her."

"Her name was never in the news." Wyatt had double-checked this morning to be sure.

"We put two and two together and so will others if they haven't already," Dade said. "It's not exactly a safe time to be connected to this family and whether you like it or not, you are."

"All the more reason to keep my distance," Wyatt said.

"That ship might've already sailed," Dade retorted, and his defenses seemed like they were flaring.

To be fair, Wyatt stood there glaring at the guy like a matador waving a red flag at a bull.

"There was an item found near the site, which links the incident to Meg's past," Wyatt informed him. Either way, he wasn't inclined to accept help from anyone in that family.

"We think we can help with the investigation and at least offer protection until the case is solved." Dade tapped the toe of his boot on the tile floor. "If you won't take our help, she should still hear the offer and decide for herself."

"Her place is with me," Wyatt interrupted.

"Agreed," Dade said. "Which is why we'd like to offer all three of you full access to one of our guest houses."

"Correct me if I'm wrong, but your father was murdered on the ranch," Wyatt stated. A twinge of regret sluiced through him the instant he saw how deeply that comment cut. Dade's split-second reaction before he recovered was a mix of hurt and wounded pride. The man was there with a peace offering. It wasn't his fault Maverick Mike was a jerk. Wyatt could concede that point.

"That's correct," Dade said.

"The sentiment is appreciated, but we'll do all right on our own." Wyatt glanced at Meg and her surprised reaction caught him off guard. Didn't she trust that he could keep them safe? "We're done here."

"Suit yourself, but if you change your mind my number is on that card I gave you," Dade said.

Dade seemed like a stand-up guy. Wyatt had to give it to him. But he could take care of his family without the help of a Butler.

Wyatt excused the three of them and headed to the truck, realizing that the sheriff had set them up.

Frustration barreled through him, but he needed to keep it in check in front of the baby.

Once inside the truck, Meg said in a reverent tone, "Mary Jane's family deserves to finally know what happened to her."

"At least they have answers. They have closure," Wyatt said. His personal affairs paled in comparison to the thought of losing a child, but he understood closure. He'd never gotten it from Maverick Mike. "I let her down." The look she shot him said that didn't matter. And that guilt would keep her from moving forward with anyone in her life. She'd never stop blaming herself for what had happened and she would always construct walls to keep people out.

"I said it once and I'll say it again. You were a kid." He caught her gaze and held it. Wyatt told himself the only reason he cared about Meg keeping everyone at a distance was for Aubrey's sake, but there was more to it than that. It was wounded pride that had him wanting her to open up a little more. Being with her brought up feelings he didn't want to acknowledge, didn't want to have for anyone.

His cell buzzed again. It was no doubt work related. He was distracted and letting things slip.

After parking at the hotel, he said, "I'll be right up."

Meg nodded. "I'll feed the baby and put her down for a nap."

As she closed the door, he checked the screen on his cell keeping one eye on her until she was safely inside the building.

There were several texts from his lawyer, Alexander Kegel. Rather than spend time texting, Wyatt called Alexander.

His lawyer picked up on the first ring. After perfunctory greetings, he said, "The shell corporation that owns the lake house is impenetrable. How much time and resource do you want to spend on this?"

"Keep digging," Wyatt instructed, which meant until the lawyer found something.

"Got it," Alexander said. "Also, I'm taking the city of Bay to court over the construction block and refusal to issue permits."

"On that one, retreat." Having a foothold in Bay wasn't as important to him now that he had a daughter. He had other priorities. "One town over, Centreville, has reached out. Let's change course. The Centreville location is still close enough the current employees will be able to commute and keep their jobs. I dug into the data last night and it turns out many of them live closer to Centreville than they do to Bay anyway. It makes more sense to go where we're wanted and appreciated."

"I'll get on the phone with Ladd as soon as we hang up," Alexander said. Hazel Ladd was the head of construction for Tiko Taco Limited.

"Good. I don't want the men standing around waiting for permits that may or may not come," Wyatt said. He'd always been the decisive, cut-his-losses type. "Let's keep them on the clock and working so they can continue to put food on the table for their families."

"We'll make it happen. Is there a specific location you're looking at?" Alexander asked.

"There's land for sale a block off the downtown area. Check into that first and make sure we have the right zoning to ease the transition," he instructed.

"Done. What else?" Alexander was his make-it-happen guy and an important part of his business. Their relationship worked because they kept it professional.

There was no gray area, no confusion.

"That's all for now." Keeping emotions out of their exchanges was the reason they worked so well together.

He'd hold on to that thought when it came to Meg.

Because his emotions had him wanting to run his finger down her generous curves and see if she still mewled with pleasure when he grazed a trail up her neck with his tongue.

With everything on the line between them, that was just dangerous and stupid.

Maintaining a safe distance was the only logical move.

Chapter Eleven

The air outside had been cold and gusty.

The baby had been fussy while Wyatt was in his truck. Did she miss her father? The thought was illogical, Meg knew that, but not entirely impossible. *Right?*

The boogeyman who had been haunting Meg for eighteen years had a name. Clayton Glass. The worst part? An internet search hadn't revealed any photos or information about him. The only thing she knew for certain was that he hadn't been the one to try to abduct Aubrey.

So, who was it?

Wyatt walked inside the suite and tension sat thickly between them.

On top of that, Meg's throat hurt and she sneezed five times in a row. It was probably just allergies with all the wind blowing every possible allergen into the area, but Meg couldn't be certain and she didn't want to risk getting the baby sick if she was going down herself.

"Do you mind holding her for a second?" Meg asked Wyatt, handing over their daughter. He took the baby from her, cradling Aubrey in his arms, looking more at ease than the last time. If Wyatt had been irresistible before, he'd jumped into a whole new stratosphere now while holding the infant against his muscled chest in such a contrast between innocence and strength.

Meg knew from experience just what his skin felt like, silk over steel. And her fingertips had reacted to grazing his skin as she'd handed over the baby.

His fierce, protective look only enhanced her attraction to him—an attraction that had no business distracting her at the moment.

"I've been reviewing my most heated cases from the past six months." She retrieved her laptop and moved onto the couch next to him. Another sneeze and she scooted to the opposite end. She cleared her throat and tried to speak again. "Hold on."

Meg set her laptop in between them before getting up and moving into the kitchenette.

"Can I take a look?" he asked.

"Absolutely not," she said a little too quickly.

"I wouldn't normally ask, believe me. I respect what you do more than you can realize. But our daughter is in danger," he continued, clearly hoping she'd have a change of heart.

After heating water in the microwave and squeezing a lemon wedge into the cup, she returned. "You're right. Technically, only employees can read those files."

"Hire me." It wasn't the worst idea.

She drummed her fingers on the side of the cup.

She sat down beside him.

"Create a board. Put me on it. That would qualify." He was right about that.

"Okay. You're right. I have to do whatever I can to ensure Aubrey's safety. I'll speak to Stephanie about the board. For now, you can fill in for her."

He stared at the screen for a long moment. "Why didn't you go to the police before?"

"About which part exactly? I get threats in this line of work," she said.

"Between those and men hitting on you, I'm not sure…" He didn't finish and it looked like anger was getting the best of him. And there was another emotion present. It looked a lot like jealousy.

Meg dismissed it as her imagination taking over or some maternal desire wishing for more from Wyatt, like a happy family. And the only reason she wished for that was for Aubrey's sake. Plus, her hormones hadn't readjusted.

Moving on.

She cradled the warm cup in her hands.

"How do you deal with this kind of abuse on a daily basis?" There was so much anger and indignation in his voice.

"It's just part of the job," she admitted on a shrug. "I fight against bullies. They push back."

"No one should have to put up with this, let alone you. You're a decent person, despite what this idiot thinks." He motioned toward the screen.

She suppressed a chuckle. "Those people are the reason my job is so important."

"What can you possibly get out of going head-to-head with...*jerks*...who can't even spell your name correctly?"

"I don't do it for them. Most of them are angry and used to getting their way because of it. To be honest, I'd rather they take their frustration out on me instead of my clients." She perched on one leg. "The kids are why I do my job." She scooted a little closer and minimized the screen to her wallpaper, which was covered in photos of smiling kids cuddling dogs or cats, or sitting on Santa's lap wearing the biggest smiles.

"These are your clients?" he asked, and his tone was much softer now.

"Yes. They deserve to have someone fighting for them, someone who won't be intimidated by an abusive or neglectful parent," she said. "That's what I do."

"It's one of the things I respected about you when we first met," he said in a low rumble of a voice. "When you talked about your work your eyes sparked, and I could tell you were doing something you believed in. I've never met anyone else with that kind of passion."

She didn't remember saying much about it before. Meg always liked to keep her professional life quiet and she could never discuss details for obvious reasons. It was easier not to mention what she did. When she really thought about it, she had opened up to Wyatt about her personal life more than she had to anyone else in her past.

Stephanie knew the most about Meg's caseload, but she'd kept her on a need-to-know basis as far as threats went. There was no reason to rile everyone up over a bully.

Wyatt maximized her email, covering the screen. "I'd like to check the list of names you gave the sheriff."

"Most of what's on there is just venting," she said. "They don't mean any of it. They're used to having a punching bag and I've taken that away from them. It's just words. They don't mean any of it."

It occurred to her that she'd just repeated the phrase, *they don't mean any of it.* Was she trying to convince herself?

"I'm not so sure and after reading a few of these, I'd like to meet some of these—" he looked to bite back a few angry words "—people personally. Especially this one." He pointed toward a name. Hector Findley.

"He's on the list," she admitted.

"How many names did you give Sawmill?" he asked.

"Seven," she said on a shrug, trying to pull off nonchalant.

"There are at least six more Hectors?" Wyatt's full lips thinned.

Aubrey stirred.

"We shouldn't talk about this in front of her," Meg said. "I read somewhere that babies are constantly reading our moods. If she feels tension every time we talk, she might think we're not getting along."

Wyatt glanced down at the baby and then his gaze bounced back to Meg. "We can do better than that."

"Is she asleep?" Wyatt asked as Meg entered the kitchenette. A half hour had passed since Meg had disappeared into the baby's room to put her down for a nap. He poured a cup of coffee and handed it to her.

"Yes, thankfully." Babies must have a sixth sense about when their parents needed to talk or get something important done, because every time Meg needed her daughter to sleep the little girl fussed instead.

Wyatt moved to the table, sat down and repositioned the screen on her laptop so that both of them could see. "I've narrowed it down to three names I think pose an actual threat."

He pointed toward the first.

"We already mentioned him." Hector. "Tell me more about his case."

"I can't do that without violating confidences," she warned. "It would be unethical. Besides I've already overlooked your digging into the files without my permission."

"Protecting your cases is important. You don't have to tell me specifics. Just why these men are writing threatening emails," he said.

"Because when I testify they'll lose people they view as their possessions," she stated matter-of-factly. "In Hector's case, he repeatedly hit his common-law wife in front of her daughter. My client is nine, Wyatt. He told her that he'd hunt them down and make her watch him kill her mother if they left him. Her mother said that he always feels bad later and that's why she stayed with him. He'd cry and tell her that he was going to get help. And then he'd be really nice to her and my client. The peace usually lasted a month, sometimes two, before something would set him off again. The mother felt like it was partly her fault. She grew up in an abusive household and came to expect it from a relationship. They'd fight. He'd go out drinking, wake the house up when he got home and repeat the cycle of abuse all over again."

His lips thinned and his eyebrows drew together, but he didn't speak.

She glanced at the second name. "Rodney

Straum. He works as a youth-group leader. My client is the only one who's come forward. Forensic evidence corroborates his story."

Wyatt white-knuckled his coffee mug and anger seethed behind his normally cool steel-gray eyes. "How do you do it?"

"What?"

"Take up cases like these? I've heard about two so far, and it's taking everything inside me not to look these jerks up and teach them a lesson about being a real man," he said.

"Hearing about the abuses that occur, that's the hard part of my job. If that's all I focused on I'd be in trouble. I mean, these stories make what I've been through seem like nothing," she admitted, realizing she'd slipped. She didn't discuss her background with anyone. Maybe he'd write it off as her experience with Mary Jane and not relate it to the emotional suffering that came after when her own mother had rejected her. "Here, let me show you something."

She moved closer to the computer, ignoring the heat skittering up her arm when her left shoulder touched his right as she repositioned to get closer to the keyboard. Showing him this would hopefully make him feel better because it was the only thing that kept her going when all she wanted to do was cry for the children involved.

"Here's an update from Alicia Rose's mother." The file opened to a smiling, healthy fourteen-year-old at summer camp. "Her biological father tortured them both. He's locked away in a place he can't hurt another woman or child, thanks to tougher laws that we lobbied for."

"She looks happy," he conceded.

"Alicia's taking hard classes at school and is an honors student. She has a close circle of friends. None of that seemed possible when she was ten years old," Meg said, and she could hear the pride in her own voice. "When these men are faced with losing control, they lash out. Anger is how they deal with life. Usually, that means they come at me."

Wyatt issued a grunt.

"I'd gladly take the brunt of a few angry emails in order to protect people who are weaker than I am," she defended. "None of those words make me lose sleep."

"Until now…" Wyatt glanced up at her. "I wish you'd told me about this sooner. You never said anything or gave me the impression anything like this was going on."

"We dated a few months. What was I supposed to do? Spill my whole life story?" she asked, but she knew it was a cop-out. A glance toward him said he knew it, too. Okay, she'd kept parts of her life from him...*most* of her life from him. Guilt stabbed at her, but she deflected. "It's not like we were serious."

Wyatt shot up out of his seat so fast his movement startled her. He raked his fingers through his bronze hair. There was enough stubble on his chin to reveal he hadn't shaved in at least twenty-four hours. "No. We weren't."

He scooped his cup off the table and refilled it with coffee.

Why did his words sting so much?

They'd had a fling. It was supposed to be a stress reliever. So, why did all her plans come back to bite her in the back side? Her fling had turned into what could've been real feelings and they'd made a baby. Neither was supposed to be on the table.

"We were both busy with our careers. We didn't have time to get to know each other any better," she said, and there was more defensiveness in her tone than she'd intended. Besides, what had been up with the fact that he only had one coffee mug at his place? Who only had *one*?

Wyatt looked at her. No, the right word was *through* her. And it looked like he was about to say something significant. Whatever it was seemed to die on his tongue. Instead, he cracked a smile and shook his head. "No. We didn't. Which makes even less sense why we have a baby together."

Okay, that hurt. "Aubrey's a beautiful little girl and none of this is her fault." Yes, she was being defensive.

"Never said it was. It's ours."

Oh, was that what he thought? That their child was a burden?

"You don't have to be involved," she defended.

The look he shot could've frozen gasoline. "Then you really don't know me."

"I'm just saying that I didn't tell you to force you to be involved or get money out of you. I have enough to take care of her," she said, hating how shaky her voice sounded.

"My child won't want for anything." His tone was final. "I don't place the blame on you for this happening."

He didn't?

"I take full responsibility," he said. "Wish you'd clued me in sooner, but we're here now. That little girl stirs something in my chest I've never felt before. She deserves to know both of her parents. She deserves to have the benefits of a father who has the means to make sure she has access to a good education and is brought up in a nice house. She deserves to have parents who find a way to get along if for no other reason than for her sake."

He was making sense and saying the words Meg thought she wanted to hear. So, why did they sting?

"We can split her expenses fifty-fifty," she said.

"With all due respect, I can do better than that." His tone was final, and she didn't like the implication that she couldn't pull her weight when it came to their child.

"We can work out those details later," she said with a warning glance.

He stood there for a long moment before he reclaimed his seat. "Tell me about Zach Brandt."

Chapter Twelve

"Brandt is bipolar and drinks to numb his pain," Meg offered. Changing the subject was probably for the best. Opening up and talking about herself, about their nonrelationship, felt like poking a bruise with a stick, pointless and painful with nothing to gain.

For Aubrey's sake, they would need to interact and be strong. If she could get to a place where her body didn't hum every time he was close, she'd be a lot happier. And there'd be a lot less stress.

"What's the story?" he asked.

"When he's up, all is well. When he's down, it gets pretty bad. Paranoia. There are no physical bruises, but once he decided that aliens were trying to read his mind so he blocked out all the windows with aluminum foil and made 'hats' from the same material in order to block transmission," she said. "He would go several days without food or water, saying that the aliens were contaminating the food supply in order to control everyone's minds."

"He sounds like a complete nut job," Wyatt said.

"Social services keeps urging him to go to the doctor. As soon as he shows the slightest bit of stability, they return his two children." Frustration nipped at her.

"This is the last person on earth who should be caring for children," Wyatt said.

"Agreed. His kids are two and four," she continued. "They're too young to fight for themselves."

"How'd you get the case?" His brow arched.

"Part of my job is to review social workers' caseloads. In their defense, they like to keep families together and they also have limited resources to work with. They can't be certain that kids who end up in foster care or with adopted families end up doing much better. Especially the ones who end up in foster care," she admitted.

"This seems like a no-brainer. Take the kids, right?" he asked.

"In this case, I agree one hundred percent.

Nothing good can come from this guy keeping his children. They're young and adoptable."

"So, basically, if you can't find parents these kids could end up passed around in the system without ever finding a real home," he said on a sharp sigh.

Meg nodded.

"Sounds hopeless if you ask me. Even if you win, they could lose." He stared hard at a point on the wall.

"How would any of them know about the ribbon? I mean, it's the *exact* color and kind of ribbon she wore the day…" A sob escaped before Meg could suppress it. She stood and turned her back to Wyatt with a mumbled apology.

She knew he'd moved behind her even before his hand touched her shoulder. His scent—a mix of outdoors and clean and masculine—filled her senses, robbing her of the ability to think for a split second. Wyatt had that effect on her, which made him dangerous. She could work with him for Aubrey's sake but, dammit, she couldn't go there with her emotions no matter how much her body trembled underneath his touch. And it did tremble.

"Surely the ribbon was in the news. Some-one could find a past article and dig up information about it," he said, and his voice was a low rumble against her hair. The only parts touching were his hand to her shoulder and yet she could feel his presence as though it was wrapped around her.

"I guess we won't know until forensics tells us," she said. It was a valid point. One they wouldn't have an answer to for a while or until they nailed the bastard and got a confession.

Her arms had goose bumps, and a trill of awareness shot through her when he closed the distance between them.

The hand on her shoulder moved her hair to one side, and he dipped his head and pressed a soft kiss on her bared shoulder. Heat flooded her and her thoughts shifted. Muscle memory had her wanting to turn around and reach for him, to feel him on top of her pressing her into the mattress. To feel safe again. It had been so long since she'd felt she could count on someone else.

It was so easy to get lost with Wyatt standing there, his lips lighting a hot trail up her neck to her ear. She could feel his warm breath sensitizing every place it touched, and her own mouth went cotton-ball dry.

"Meg," he said, and his voice was gravelly.

The baby cried and Meg's heart lurched. She pushed off Wyatt and mumbled another apology as she darted toward the hallway. The thought of anything happening to her girl—no matter how improbable that was given she was being watched over by the two of them 24/7—caused her heart to jump into her throat.

Meg raced to the crib in time for another ear-piercing scream.

"What it is?" Wyatt said, and there was so much concern in his voice.

Meg made it to her daughter before the next burst of tears sprang from the little girl's face. Aubrey was fine. A glance at the clock told her everything she needed to know about what was going on with her daughter. "She's hungry."

"Right. Milk. I'll make a bottle." There was so much relief in his tone. He disappeared, his deep baritone a cover for how shaken he'd been earlier. A relationship between her and Wyatt wouldn't amount to more than hot sex...and the sex would be smoking hot. But real feelings? Sexual chemistry was one thing and they had that in spades. And that's where it skidded to a halt. Wyatt wasn't capable of more, she reasoned.

Except when it came to Aubrey.

His feelings toward his daughter seemed genuine enough, especially with the determined look he got every time he talked about keeping Aubrey safe. She had no doubt that he'd do everything in his power to protect that little girl and give her a bright future.

Meg prayed it would be enough to keep their daughter safe through this nightmare.

She gently bounced up and down, soothing Aubrey as best she could. The little girl cried, but even that was a sweet sound to Meg. Being able to hold her daughter after almost losing her...

The thought of anything happening to Aubrey caused hot tears to spill down Meg's cheeks.

Wyatt returned a few minutes later with a bottle.

"I can feed her," he offered after getting a good look at Meg.

Covering the fact she was crying with a cough, she blamed her watery eyes on allergies. "I've got this."

She would have to learn to share Aubrey in the very near future. Now, though, she couldn't go there. Meg needed to hold her daughter in her arms.

Aubrey latched on to the nipple immediately and settled with the first drop of warm liquid in her mouth. Meg walked to the bed and perched on the edge, gazing down at her little miracle.

A dark feeling settled over her as thoughts of Mary Jane's kidnapping resurfaced.

Had her kidnapper been working with a partner? Or had past news coverage of the crime brought a different kind of boogeyman out from under the bed? One who wanted to see Meg suffer before killing her?

WYATT MIGHT BE brand-new at this parenting thing but he knew Meg well enough to realize that she needed to hold her daughter. He closed the door behind him and moved into the kitchen.

After pouring a cup of coffee—because he could face facts, there'd be no sleeping tonight—he moved back to the laptop. His own work was piling up, but Alexander was handling the bigger tasks and nothing was more important to Wyatt than keeping that little girl in the next room safe.

His emotions had gotten the best of him earlier. Emotions…sexual chemistry? Hell, he couldn't tell them apart anymore when it came to his reaction to Meg. The two had had great sex last year. No question. But he was beginning to realize just how precious little he really knew about her.

In her defense, there was no way to work into conversation the kind of horror she'd been through as a child. And he could see why she'd want to distance herself from all of that and never bring it up again.

Then there was his complicated family dynamic to deal with. His personal business was being splashed all over every front page of most every news outlet. Maverick Mike Butler was big news. Even more reason Wyatt didn't want or need to be included in that family.

Since going down that route was as productive as trying to milk a cat, he refocused on the screen. Families were complicated as hell. The thought of his own daughter going through any of that nonsense sent a wave of rage surging through him.

He didn't know the first thing about parenting, and his role model for being a father was a complete failure at the job. Further, Wyatt didn't know the first place to begin to figure it out. His mother had been a decent person. Poverty hadn't given her a lot of options, and he'd often wondered how on earth she'd met Maverick Mike let alone struck up an affair with the man. But, then, based on his reputation, Maverick Mike had taken up with quite a few women and hadn't seemed to mind walking away.

Anger was a hot poker pressed to Wyatt's chest thinking about a rich man taking advantage of his mother. And yet part of him wondered how that could've been. She'd been one of the strongest people he'd known, making it difficult to imagine anyone could get one over on her.

He wondered how Butler had taken the news that Wyatt's mother was pregnant. How vulnerable his mother had had to be to tell Butler in the first place.

Now that was ironic.

Wyatt flashed to the morning Meg had told him about Aubrey. He'd been about the biggest jerk a man could be under the circumstances. Damn. It was becoming hard to condemn his own father considering how Wyatt had handled the conversation.

Meg was proud, like his mother. Had his mother refused support, too? Had Butler even bothered to offer?

Maybe that's what set Wyatt apart from the

Butler family. He took responsibility for his actions. No amount of arguing would stop him from taking care of his child. He expected nothing less of any guy who called himself a real man.

"Find anything interesting?" Meg's voice cut through his heavy thoughts. He glanced up to see the baby being gently held over Meg's shoulder as she bounced and patted the little girl's back.

"I need to say something," he started. Finding the right words was hell. He settled on, "I'm sorry I wasn't here for all of it."

"It's not your fault," she said without hesitation, and he appreciated her letting him off the hook so easily. He couldn't.

"Yes, it is."

Now she turned to him and he half expected her to check his forehead for fever.

"Hold on. Before you assume I've lost it, hear me out. If I'd been a better man, you would've come to me sooner," he said.

Meg looked floored.

"I appreciate you being willing to take the fall for that, but I should've let you know the minute I found out," she argued.

"You would've if I'd made you feel safe enough."

MEG ALMOST DIDN'T know what to say in response. Was that true? Could she so easily shift blame to Wyatt for her actions?

No. Because if she let him take the fall for this, then what else would she blame others for?

"I appreciate the sentiment. I really do. But we're going to have to agree to disagree on this. I should've been stronger. I panicked. Not that I don't love Aubrey with all my heart. I do. But I completely freaked out when I learned I was pregnant and backed off," she said.

"Because I didn't make you feel safe."

Okay, repeating those words weren't going to make them come true. Plus, they riled her up. Call her a feminist, but his actions didn't dictate hers, she thought stiffly. But she could see that he was making an effort to take some responsibility for where they were emotionally and she respected that. Plus, they did need to find common ground for Aubrey's sake. Learn to work together better so their daughter didn't pay the price.

"I appreciate what you're saying. And I want to work together, too. If we get along and make joint decisions, Aubrey's life will be better for it." Aubrey would never feel she'd been responsible for her parents not getting along or being married. So much for feminism. Meg could bring up her daughter on her own. Aubrey would always feel loved by her mother...

And that stopped her in her mental tracks.

How great would it be for Aubrey to feel loved by her father, too?

Meg had to admit the notion brought warmth to her chest and a sense of calm came over her. Having someone else for Aubrey to count on seemed almost too good to be true. Meg had no memories of her own father, so this was new territory. He'd ditched both her and her mother long before Meg was old enough to recall anything about him. Pain pierced her chest.

"What's wrong?" Wyatt was staring at her. One of his brows was arched like he was looking at a puzzle he couldn't quite figure out.

"I'm okay," she said quickly. A little too quickly. "Look, I'm new at this whole 'having two involved parents' thing, so forgive me if I'm no good at it."

"Same goes here."

"Your father was Maverick Mike Butler," she said. "And you never shared that with me when we dated before."

"Would it have made a difference?"

"No. But that's not the point." She wished he'd trusted her enough to tell her.

"Then I'm lost. What is?" he asked, that same puzzled look on his face. He really had no idea what she was talking about.

"Forget it," she said. "Let's just promise to keep working together until we figure this out. I'm sure coparenting is like anything else you do for the first time. It takes practice in order to get it right."

Being in a room with Wyatt when her nerve endings hummed with need probably wasn't the best idea. It had been a long time since she'd had sex and not because of an outdated belief that single mothers should stay home 24/7 but because the reality of caring for a baby left her too exhausted to leave the house.

And then there was Wyatt. Sex with him had been over-the-top incredible at least in part because of their physical chemistry. Wyatt was sex in a bucket with his easy charm, devastating smile and brilliant mind. His sense of humor and good looks had been so good at seducing her. She'd let her emotions get away from her on something that was supposed to be a stress-relieving, take-time-out-for-herself fling.

The minute she'd realized her mistake in developing real feelings for him, she'd retreated. She could see now that she'd hurt his feelings, which caught her off guard. Or maybe he was just still stinging from her rejection. She highly doubted that Wyatt was the type of guy to lick his wounds for too long when it came to any woman.

Yet, she couldn't deny there was something she couldn't quite put her finger on that seemed genuine about his emotions. It had to be more than her wishing it to be true.

Chapter Thirteen

Meg needed to keep up her guard. Experience had taught her that she had the power to hurt others she was close to, break them, really. Like after Mary Jane's abduction when her own mother started drinking. She'd lost her job and then their home. Nothing had been the same afterward and Meg knew that her mother had secretly blamed her. And that was ironic, too, because Meg already blamed herself.

The new "uncle," who had had so much promise, according to her mother, cut his losses. He'd left town for a new job and said he'd send for them. Not long after, his cell number didn't work and he all but disappeared.

Meg had watched her mother sink into a deeper depression, drink more, stay in bed long past morning. It wasn't long before social services started regular visits. Her mother had been able to get her act together enough to apply for welfare and keep up appearances, but their relationship was never the same.

The day after Meg had graduated from high school, her mother took off. She left two hundred dollars along with a note, telling her she'd be better off on her own.

The two hadn't spoken since.

Meg could place blame on her mother for leaving. Having stuck around for the next eight years after the life-changing incident had seemed to drain the life out of the woman.

Speaking of which, Meg picked up her phone and called Stephanie.

"I just wanted to call and see how you're doing," Meg said. Her friend's voice was a welcome relief from heavier thoughts.

"Better," Stephanie said. "I appreciate everything you've done for me, but I can go back—"

"It's best for you to stay where you are for now at Wyatt's place," Meg said. When Stephanie didn't respond, Meg added, "As a favor to me if nothing else."

The line was quiet.

"Stephanie?" Meg's fear radar jacked up.

"I'm here," she reassured. "I'm sorry about your friend."

Meg hadn't checked online, but she feared her story had been slapped across headlines by now. The sheriff wouldn't release an important detail but there were others at the scene of Aubrey's attempted kidnapping. "Thank you."

She cringed, waiting for the accusations it had been her fault or the judgment that came with knowing she was there and couldn't remember or help.

"It's unfair that happened to both of you. And so young." There was kindness and compassion in Stephanie's voice.

"Did you get any rest?" her friend asked.

"Some," she responded. "But I'm more worried about you right now."

"Me? I'm fine. I slept twelve hours last night and woke feeling the best I have in months. But what I'm hearing from you is that you haven't slept yet." Stephanie knew her a little better than Meg was comfortable with at the moment.

Meg stood with her back against the counter. "Not really. But I did lie down for a while and feel more refreshed."

"How's the baby?" Hearing how Stephanie's voice morphed from overprotective mama to basically a glop of goo almost made Meg chuckle. Under different circumstances, she would do just that but nothing had been funny in her life for a long time.

"She's been great under the circumstances," Meg admitted.

"And the cowboy?" There was a hint of admiration in her voice.

"You mean Wyatt?"

"Yeah, that guy. How's he doing with all this?" Stephanie asked.

"How do you know he's still with me?" Meg didn't mask her surprise.

"I saw the way he looked at Aubrey," she said.

Meg could admit to witnessing the same. There was something warm and reassuring about another human being loving her daughter so much. Meg's world had consisted of her mother and no one else. When she lost her mother to drinking—drinking that was Meg's fault—the world had tumbled down around her. A surprising tear sprang to her eye just thinking about the past.

Meg wanted—no—*needed* so much more for her daughter. She saw her daughter surrounded by people who loved her. She saw birthday parties with kids playing and laughing. She saw Wyatt doting on their daughter.

And a little piece of her heart saw a wedding band on his finger.

It was a childish fantasy to think that a child's parents had to be married for life to feel complete. All Aubrey really needed was two parents to love her. It didn't matter whether they lived in the same house or not. Heck, some kids thrived with one involved parent, and Meg had seen all too many cases where one parent was a detriment to the child.

Meg had already made up her mind that her past relationship with Wyatt had nothing to do with Aubrey. How silly was that? He was Aubrey's father. And the two of them were certainly going to have to continue to work at figuring out how to parent together.

It was probably a mix of almost losing her daughter coupled with the emotions of the pending holiday and the past being dredged up that had Meg ready to abandon reason for fantasy. Aubrey had a mother who loved her and that was so much more than Meg had had.

"You know she can stay with me here at the complex," Stephanie offered. "Since you didn't hear me the first time I said it."

"Sorry. I'm distracted." She faked a yawn. "I don't want to draw any more heat to Ava's operation. She's already doing us a huge favor by taking you until this…situation…is cleared up."

"It's quiet there," Stephanie conceded. "You should lie back down and seriously try to sleep. You know she'll have you up every few hours."

"I will." Meg said before ending the call. Why was it that hospital nurses and pretty much every caring-for-a-newborn blog told new mothers to sleep when the baby slept? If Meg did that she wouldn't get any work done, her house would be a complete wreck and she'd—

"What's wrong?" Wyatt stepped into the kitchen, fresh from a shower. His curly hair seemed darker when it was wet and she didn't even want to think about the fact that he'd been naked a few minutes ago.

She cleared her dry throat in order to speak. "Nothing. What makes you think something's wrong?"

He glanced at her hand and then locked on to her gaze. "You're white-knuckling your cell. Did something happen?"

"Oh." Meg tried to force her fingers to relax on the phone. When that didn't work, she set it on the counter. Turning to grab a mug and make a cup of tea, she heard Wyatt walk up behind her. She felt his presence when he got close and her body hummed with electricity.

She took in a sharp breath when she realized how close he was—a breath that ushered in his fresh-from-the-shower masculine scent.

"I'm sorry about earlier," he said, and he was so close she wouldn't have to move much more than an inch to be body-to-body with him.

"It was a mistake." He might be standing so near that her heart thundered in her chest and her pulse pounded, but she didn't want to give away the effect he had on her. She refused to maintain eye contact as she turned to face him.

He lifted her chin up.

"I've been thinking a lot about that kiss," he said, and her gaze locked on to his.

"It shouldn't have happened," she said, figuring he was about to say the same. This way, she could head him off at the pass.

"I'm glad it did," he said, surprising her.

"Why?" she asked.

"Because it reminded me that I'm alive. I'm human. I make mistakes—"

She held up her hand, effectively cutting him off before he could go all macho on her. "Apologizing for kissing me isn't necessary and it might just hurt my feelings."

"Good."

Meg made the mistake of locking eyes with him again. "So you want to make me feel bad?"

"I didn't say that." He issued a sharp sigh. "I had no plans to apologize. I'm relieved that saying sorry isn't required."

"Why's that?"

"Because I don't want to hurt you," he said. "And I'm no good at feelings."

"You already have hurt me," she countered, but there was no emotion behind the words.

"By doing this?" He dipped his head and captured her bottom lip gently between his teeth.

"Yes." She drew out the word as he released it. His breath smelled like her favorite peppermint toothpaste and a unique mix of all that was Wyatt, because she was certain her brand didn't taste like this straight out of the tube.

Wyatt took a step toward her, closing the small gap between them, and her body stiffened. He looked into her eyes; his were hungry and primal, and she gasped as their bodies pressed against each other. His chest was a wall of muscled steel with a silky exterior, and she should know because her hands gripped him in an almost laughable attempt to push him away.

Instead, her fingers dug into his shoulders. Instinct took over and she pulled him toward her.

"What about this?" He dipped his head again, skimming his lips along the line of her collarbone, her neck, across her jawline…

Until he found her mouth and hovered just out of reach. Her lips stung with a need for contact. Every uniquely feminine part warmed, and there was such a strong sense of urgency building inside her, like a tsunami that would obliterate everything in its path when it made landfall. And yet she didn't care about the destruction it would leave. Not when he was this close and her senses overrode rational thought.

Wyatt looked at her one more time with a question in his eyes. His hands came up and cupped her face as they made contact.

She nodded so slightly that she could tell he almost missed it. Almost. Until she realized his pupils dilated right before he kissed her.

Meg parted her lips to allow better access, and he took the invitation immediately, sliding his tongue inside. His tongue slicked across hers. He tasted even better than she remembered and her body cried out for more contact. He seemed ready to take it slow, and that only built up the wave gathering momentum inside her. Her body was strung tight with tension.

Meg dropped her hands and ran her fingers along the strong wall of his chest, letting her fingertips linger on his long, lean muscles. He took a half step back and pulled his shirt over his head in a heartbeat, tossing it to the floor. Speaking of things being better than she remembered, his body was in a whole new stratosphere of muscled strength. She smoothed her palms over his pecs as he unbuttoned her blouse.

She shrugged out of it, and a moment later the thin material joined his on the floor.

A primal grunt issued from Wyatt as he took in her almost fully bared breasts. His thumb ran across the lace of her flesh-colored bra, sending goose bumps racing up her arms. Awareness skittered across her sensitized skin as he outlined the thin material. Her nipples pebbled and her breasts swelled from needing contact.

Urgency was building from a deep place inside her, sending impulses shooting through her sensitized body.

"You're even more beautiful, Meg," he said, trailing his finger around her beaded nipple. He rolled one in between his thumb and forefinger, causing her breasts to swell with need, her body to hum.

The words were appreciated but unnecessary because the look of appreciation in his eyes stirred more emotion and physical attraction.

Without waiting for him to take the lead, she unzipped her jeans, popped the snap and wiggled out of them until she was standing there in her bra and underwear. Under any other circumstance this would be awkward.

With Wyatt, she felt adored and at ease.

Of course, his charm had been all too good at seducing her before, and that same skilled smile overtook his lips now. She pushed up to her toes and kissed him, pressing her body to his before he could say anything.

He leaned against her until her bottom met the hard countertop. Her hands flew to the buttons on his jeans.

It took two seconds flat for him to join her and have his jeans, boxers included, added to the clothing pile on the floor.

His erection pulsed and strained against her midsection as he freed her from her silky bra. She stepped out of her panties next and he grunted another sound of appreciation. Before either could talk themselves out of what was going to happen next, she hopped onto the countertop and wrapped her legs around his toned stomach. He stepped toward her, *into* her, as she guided him inside her slick heat.

He cupped her breasts as she worked her hips to allow him better access. And then his hands dropped to her bottom as he thrust inside her, taking her breath away. He looked into her eyes as he drove deeper.

"I missed *this*. *You*," he said in a low, gravelly voice.

"Me, too, Wyatt," she said, wishing that it could last longer than today. Knowing that was unrealistic.

In that moment, she didn't care a bit. She tightened her grip around his waist and pressed her body against his. In a swift movement, her bottom left the hard granite and he was carrying her into the master bedroom. The baby slept in the room next door.

They both came down hard on the bed, entangled in each other's arms and legs. Both laughed, but all Meg could really feel was how good he felt on top of her, his solid weight pressing her deeper into the mattress. This was home to her and in that moment she knew he felt the same way. He paused long enough to retrieve a condom and sheathe himself.

He looked into her eyes with so much adoration, her heart stirred, and that was dangerous ground. Sex was one thing, an easy thing when it came to Wyatt. Emotions were a slippery slope they had yet to figure out how to navigate effectively.

Wyatt pressed his lips to hers and drove his tongue inside her mouth in an air-grabbing kiss. All reason, all hesitation flew out the window. All that mattered was the fleeting feeling Meg had right now—love. *Love?*

Meg clasped her legs around Wyatt and bucked him deeper. He responded in kind until they met a fever pitch reaching faster and higher, their bodies so tense she felt like a bomb about to detonate. Meg's body was alive with sensation she hadn't felt in so long…since the last time with Wyatt.

He matched her stride for stride as they climbed to the summit together and stood at the edge not yet ready to trust and completely let go. Need overtook every rational thought… a need to release all the tension in her body.

Instinct and need took over, and Meg relinquished control. She raised to a fever pitch until she could no longer fight the pressure. She dove off the cliff into pure pleasure and sensation, and fireworks being lit at the same time.

Wyatt's body, still taut, drove deeper until, with a primal noise of release, he detonated inside her. She could feel his erection pulsing and releasing until his body seemed drained.

He rolled onto one side and positioned her in the crook of his arm. His breathing was coming out in jagged gasps.

"I'm done for," he said through raspy breaths. "In serious trouble."

She had no idea what he meant by that.

But she hoped it meant more than it probably did.

Curled against him, Meg drifted off into a deep sleep.

Meg couldn't be sure how much time had passed when a sudden noise startled her awake. Meg sat bolt upright. She scanned the dark room and patted the empty bed.

Wyatt was gone.

Chapter Fourteen

The email from Alexander had come in while Meg was still sleeping. The offer he'd made on the land in Centreville had been accepted; permits were being fast-tracked, and construction would be back on track in the new location in a week. Still, no word on the lake house, though.

At least part of his life was coming together...

Meg burst out of the bedroom. The baby in Wyatt's arms jerked awake.

"What is it?" he asked, holding as still as he could considering every instinct had him wanting to jump up and run toward her. She had come out of that room so fast a split-second fear that someone would fly out behind her with a gun struck him.

"I thought you were gone," she said through

gasps of air. "A noise woke me. You weren't there. I freaked."

Sweat beaded on her forehead and he could see that she was trembling.

"I'm right here," he said. "I'm not going anywhere without telling you first."

He had to qualify that last part, because there would come a time when they wouldn't spend so much time around each other. That would be a good thing from the standpoint of the investigation. It would mean Meg and the baby were safe and could get back to their old routine. But what about Wyatt?

The thought of going back to his house in Austin alone sent a strange burning sensation shooting through his chest.

Maybe he could stick around. Put some furniture in that house next door to hers that he'd rented and spend a little time there? It wasn't a horrible thought.

Besides, his daughter was beginning to feel more and more natural in his arms, and he needed to learn to take care of her on his own. He could do bottles and a diaper, but there was a whole lot more involved in caring for a baby than that.

But, hey, getting a diaper on her correctly

and securely was something to be proud of. At this point, he'd take all the little wins he could get. He had a feeling this parenting thing wasn't going to be easy. Unlike at work, he could tell people what to do and they would listen. The bundle in his arms had complete control over him, and all he could do—and surprisingly wanted to do—was let her take the lead.

Meg stood there, rooted to her spot, and he could tell she needed more reassurance.

"I'm here. I'm not leaving." That was absolute truth. Not until they had answers.

Watching his daughter sleep, he vowed to give her mother the same peace of mind. They were getting close to finding the truth. Wyatt could feel it. Learning the name from her past and finding out the man was in prison had at first felt like a setback. Not anymore, and he wanted to discuss his theories with her once the baby was down for the night.

"Let's get out of here and grab a bite to eat," he said. There was an out-of-the-way restaurant he'd spotted on the way back from the sheriff's office. Meg needed a good meal and something that felt normal. She needed a fresh perspective and so did he. Taking a break and looking at a problem from a new perspective had always helped him find the answers.

"Okay." She dragged her hand through her hair. "I'll just get dressed."

"THIS WAS A good idea," Meg said, after taking the last bite of chicken-fried steak on her plate. "I didn't think I'd be able to stomach anything."

Taking a break from the heaviness of the afternoon was good. They could both use a fresh perspective.

And, besides, Wyatt liked making Meg happy. A decent meal was the least he could give her after all she'd been through.

The baby had slept through the entire meal and tension had slowly eased from Meg's facial features. He picked up the bill the server had dropped off. "I'll take care of this."

"Before we go, I need to use the restroom," Meg said, scanning the room. It was a habit he'd noticed when they'd dated last year. She'd checked the exits of every new restaurant he'd taken her to. At first, he'd wondered if it was just one of her quirks. Then, he'd considered the possibility that she was being overly vigilant with the spate of random crimes on the news in the Austin area. Had he been dead wrong. Her paranoia took on a whole new meaning and he understood so much more of her for knowing about her past.

"I'll take Aubrey," he said, picking up the baby carrier that plugged right into a base forming a secure car seat.

"Okay. I'll meet you out front," she said.

Wyatt handled the bill and walked out to the truck. The air was still chilly, but sun promised to show tomorrow if he could believe the weatherman.

The baby didn't so much as budge as the carrier clicked into place, secured in the back seat.

Until a scream shattered the night air.

Out of his peripheral vision, he saw commotion. He scanned the parking lot of the restaurant. Meg came into focus. A man had her arms jacked up behind her and the glint of metal in the sunlight said there was a gun to her temple.

Wyatt bit back a curse. Make a move and the man could squeeze the trigger faster than Wyatt could literally take a breath. Not to mention the guy could hit Aubrey if he pulled off a shot in Wyatt's direction. Who was this guy anyway? It had to be one of the fathers from her work. Right? Hector? Zach Brandt?

Fighting every instinct inside his body urging him to make a move toward the attacker, he shielded Aubrey with the truck door.

Meg didn't struggle.

"You don't want to do this," Wyatt warned.

"Stay back or she's dead, man." The guy's voice had a hysterical edge to it.

"Listen to Jonathon." Meg winced as the attacker twisted her arms even further behind her back. "Please. Wyatt. Don't follow me. Take care of her."

Jonathon Fjord. Mary Jane's brother. The sheriff had mentioned his deputies were looking for him, and now it made sense as to why he'd gone missing. Had he been plotting revenge? Waiting?

Another thought struck. Meg had said that he'd tried to approach her over the summer at the supermarket. She would've been pretty far along in her pregnancy. Seeing that could've driven him over the edge if he'd been harboring feelings against her all this time. The event, according to Meg, had traumatized him to the point he couldn't function in a normal environment again.

Anger bit through Wyatt.

Tough situation or not, none of this was Meg's fault. She'd been just as much a victim.

Her innocence had been stripped that day and Jonathon was too twisted to see it.

How could he let this guy take the woman he loved—loved? Yes, loved.

Without her, nothing in his life made sense. He'd confirmed with one kiss what he'd suspected last year. He was in love with Meg.

But what were his options?

Make a move now and the guy might just pull the trigger. Possibly kill Meg. Aubrey would be without a mother...

Damn.

He couldn't go there. Not even hypothetically.

Plus, there was the other possibility that Jonathon might take aim at the truck and strike Aubrey. If he could trade himself for Meg and know that she'd be safe, no problem.

There was no way he would put their daughter in jeopardy and Meg wouldn't want him to. His mind was spinning with bad options.

In every scenario he came up with, someone he cared about ended up dead. Unless Meg could overpower the guy and somehow knock the gun out of his hand. Wyatt couldn't get to them from this distance unless she made a move and distracted Fjord.

Wyatt had to wait, be ready if an opportunity presented itself. So, instead of taking action, he stood there with an almost overwhelming feeling of helplessness.

One-on-one, Jonathon would go down. No doubt about it. Wyatt didn't doubt his skills for a second. But his attention was splintered between Meg and Aubrey.

Jonathon had the upper hand in this scenario.

Fjord said something to Meg that Wyatt couldn't make out. She winced as his grip seemed to tighten around her neck.

"Don't follow us, Wyatt. He'll kill me," she said with certainty. "Call the sheriff and the second he sees a law enforcement vehicle anywhere near us, he'll kill me. And if you try to follow us, he'll kill me."

Could he trail them without being caught? Not with Aubrey. It was too dangerous.

Standing there, frustration bit sharp lines into his gut.

Wyatt bit back a curse as the two walked around the corner, disappearing from view. He phoned the sheriff but the call went into voicemail. Wyatt texted the details of what had happened and the location before putting his phone on vibrate. His biggest fear was that Jonathon was going to kill her anyway. Why he hadn't done it already caused Wyatt to scratch his head. *Because he wants her to feel his pain.*

Wyatt was reaching for a sliver of hope and the only one he found was in the thought Jonathon wouldn't kill her immediately.

Starting his truck would bring unwanted and dangerous attention, so he unstrapped Aubrey and cradled her against his chest. Could he get a visual on them, some kind of direction, without being seen?

If Aubrey made a single noise, it could be game over for her mother.

His strides were purposeful and silent as he closed in on the restaurant. Could he get around the corner in time? Could he get the make and model of the car? A license plate?

The answer was no. But what if he had? Then what?

That's where he hit a wall. The answer dawned on him as he circled back to the truck. He couldn't do any of this alone. He grabbed his cell and the wrinkled business card from inside his dash where he'd shoved it the other night.

And then he phoned the only person who could assist and said a prayer he remembered from childhood that he hadn't burned the bridge with the few folks he knew in Cattle Barge.

The call went to voice mail.

"I need your help." Those four words rolled off his tongue easily now, and he found, with the right motivation, they weren't difficult at all to say.

Wyatt ended the call and tried to think of someone else. There'd been no response to from the sheriff. There was no one else he confided in or could rely on. He'd constructed walls so high no one could climb over and he couldn't see out anymore.

Damn. Damn. Damn.

He white-knuckle gripped his phone.

His phone vibrated in his hand.

Wyatt recognized the number from the card. Dade Butler.

"Does your offer of help still stand?" Wyatt immediately asked.

"Everyone's here and ready to do whatever it takes to help. What do you need?" Dade responded without hesitation.

MEG'S HEAD POUNDED. It was pitch-black. She struggled to move against the bindings on her wrists. Her hands were numb. Trying to move made everything hurt.

Trying to scream did no good. Her mouth was covered with something…duct tape?

Memories crashed down.

Mary Jane's brother. Jonathon was responsible for attempting to kidnap Aubrey. But why? What did he have to gain?

Revenge?

Did he hate Meg that much?

A light flipped on and she gasped. A quick scan of the room revealed furniture but no person. Where was Jonathon? She was in some kind of container with no windows. A train car turned into a home? She'd seen things like this on TV. Weren't they on those small-house shows where people were looking for inexpensive places to live?

Struggling against her bindings, a voice from behind stopped her. *His voice.*

"You don't deserve to have the kind of life that was taken from my sister," Jonathon said, and he sounded almost hysterical.

Fear shot through her as she tried to work the bindings on her arms.

How many times had she wished she could make it up to the family? That she could've traded places with Mary Jane that day? Survivor's guilt had plagued her since then, stopping her from ever letting herself get close to anyone else.

But Aubrey didn't deserve this. That little girl needed her mother and, somehow, Meg would figure out a way to get home to her.

Wyatt flashed in her thoughts, too. The idea of losing him, of never seeing him again, hit like a physical punch that winded her.

One thing was clear. Arguing her case would do no good. Not even if her mouth wasn't taped shut. Jonathon wouldn't listen. He'd gone to too much trouble to get her, had exposed his identity in the process, and she wondered if either would make it out of this situation alive. He could kill her and then what? Go on the run for the rest of his life? Hide? How did that punish Meg for her best friend's death? And why come after her now after all these years?

She worked her lips trying to make a break in the seal as tears streamed down her cheeks, praying this wouldn't be the place where her life ended.

The thought of not seeing Aubrey again, of her daughter growing up without a mother, stabbed needles of pain through her.

On her side, tears dripped onto the cold concrete flooring.

There was no doubt that she was in some remote location. Most likely somewhere no one would think to look for her.

Had Wyatt done as she asked and stayed put? Part of her wished he hadn't and that he would burst into the room any minute with the sheriff and a few deputies at his side. She'd told him not to follow them and, really, he'd had no choice.

She didn't blame him. He'd done the right thing by Aubrey, and Meg was grateful to see how much he loved that little girl. It was an odd thought but mattered so much to her heart to know Aubrey was going to have a loving parent to care for her if…

Struggling against the bindings, Meg shook with anger and fear and outrage.

"Hold still," Jonathon commanded. She could hear him behind her doing something but couldn't tell what it was.

Like hell she would roll over and let him do whatever he wanted to her without fighting back.

He was going to kill her anyway. What was the difference if she angered him?

Meg fought harder, worked harder.

A piece of tape lifted at the corner of her mouth.

"You don't want to do this, Jonathon," she managed to get out. Her lungs burned from lack of oxygen, and even fresh air hurt as she drew it in.

"Don't you dare say my name," he said, and she could hear his footsteps on the concrete flooring coming toward her.

"She wouldn't want this. We were best friends," Meg said, biding her time until he got closer. Maybe she could wheel around and knock him off his feet. With her hands and feet bound he clearly had the advantage, but if she could knock him off balance, maybe she could do some damage before he killed her and tossed her body away.

"Friends?" The one word came out so shrill it sounded like a trapped animal. And when she really thought about it, he had been trapped in his own mind, his own sorrow.

"Doing this won't bring her back," she said. "And it won't bring peace."

Cold, hard metal pressed against the side of her head behind her ear. All she could think about was Aubrey and Wyatt. At least they had each other. Her daughter wouldn't grow up alone without love. Meg had seen the love in his eyes when he'd been holding their daughter. Part of her wanted to believe he'd had that same look the other day when they'd kissed for the first time since reuniting.

"Mary Jane is dead because of you," he ground out.

"I didn't hurt her. I would never do that," she managed to say on a gasp. Adrenaline spiked and her body trembled from the boost. A knee came down hard on her arm, pinning it to her side. There was no way out and the room felt like it was shrinking. Her lungs clawed for air and she fought to stay conscious. She wanted her last thoughts to be about Wyatt and their daughter, not this creep.

And her sweet friend, Mary Jane.

"She was my best friend," Meg said one more time.

Jonathon's laugh turned to a seething anger.

"Blame me all you want, but I didn't do anything," she said. "Believe me, I wish it had been me that day. That I was the one who'd been taken and not her."

The barrel of the gun traced around her ear

and then her forehead, moving her hair away from her face.

"That makes two of us," he said bitterly. There was so much venom in his voice that it seemed no amount of reason could penetrate his hatred for her.

She closed her eyes and prepared for the crack-of-a-bullet sound as the weapon fired. The burst of fire. The explosion when the bullet pierced her skull.

Where she thought there would be panic, anger flooded her, instead. Anger that life had handed her a terrible fate early on that had led her to this place with Mary Jane's brother. Anger that her life might be taken away in an instant and she might not be around for her daughter. Anger for the fact that she'd never know if Wyatt could truly love her since they wouldn't be given a chance. She thought she'd heard him say it when they'd made love. She should've been brave enough to ask, to take the life she wanted and not let go.

And the life she wanted was a family with Wyatt and their daughter.

Meg bucked her body, trying to fight against the certain death hovering.

"Be still," Jonathon commanded. At this point, what did it matter?

"Why? So you can enjoy killing me?" she shot back.

A grunt was issued with a blow to her back. A boot tip?

Meg rolled onto her back. "Look at me when you do it. Mary Jane wouldn't have wanted this. She would be ashamed of you."

Jonathon backhanded her across the cheek and it felt like her eye might pop out.

"Killing me won't change anything," she repeated. "We can't get Mary Jane back no matter how much we wish we could."

"Which is exactly why you're going to suffer," he said.

"She wouldn't want that. Not that you care." Meg was pushing the boundary, but he needed to hear the words again and again until they broke through. "I wish I could've changed things. Been able to remember and give the police a description. But hurting me doesn't punish Clayton Glass. He's already in Huntsville. And when this over, you'll be joining him."

"How do you know who took my sister?" Jonathon's shock twisted his face into angry lines.

There had been no pleading in her tone. She had been stating simple fact.

"Forget it. You're making this up to confuse the issue. You shouldn't have been outside that day," he said. "Mary Jane wasn't allowed and you convinced her to play. Her death is your fault."

"I did nothing of the sort," she defended, for all the good it would do. He'd made up his mind. His sister's death was on her.

Anger flared his nostrils as he straddled her and smacked her again. His legs were like vise grips. "You're a liar."

"Which would still be better than killing someone for the wrong reason," she retorted, and she could tell that his anger was rising. "Mary Jane loved you, Jonathon. You were her big brother. She idolized you."

He stilled as though he was considering her words.

And then his gaze bore down on her.

"You're trying to distract me." He belted her again and this time she spit blood.

"Jonathon, think about what you're about to do—"

"Enough," he ground out. And then he replaced the duct tape, securing it over her already raw lips. "You have to pay for what you did."

Meg tensed as the gun barrel pressed between her eyes.

"IT WAS HIM. The face from the sketch. I couldn't see it before. The sketch made his nose too big and the hair was off but I do now that I know," Wyatt said to the sheriff as he burst into his office.

"Jonathon Fjord," Sawmill said with a bowed head. "Mary Jane's brother."

"He headed west from the restaurant parking lot," Wyatt informed. "At least I think. I checked east and didn't see anyone."

Sawmill made an announcement over the radio, alerting his deputies. Next, he called Janis in and asked her to put out a Be on the Lookout, or BOLO, so that all law-enforcement personnel would be watching.

"What do we do next?" Wyatt asked.

"There's nothing to do but wait." Sawmill shot him a sympathetic look. Wyatt didn't need the man's sympathy. He needed to know where Jonathon was taking Meg.

At least she'd been alive, and he figured Jonathon was keeping her alive for a reason. There was some measure of reassurance there.

That was more than an hour ago. Time was running out.

"How well do you know this person?" Wyatt asked.

"I spoke to the family's neighbors. They described him as a quiet and polite young man. They were in shock he could be involved in anything remotely like this," the sheriff supplied. "Mary Jane's parents moved to the outskirts of town after her disappearance and mostly kept to themselves over the years. We had to do a little tracking to find them. They'd changed their names to avoid being dragged into interviews every time interest in the story picked up again."

"I'm guessing since her brother moved away last year no one suspected him," Wyatt said.

The sheriff nodded.

"What about his parents? Would they have any idea where he'd take her?" Wyatt paced around Sheriff Sawmill's office. He'd made more laps than he cared to count.

"I have a deputy heading over there now, but we didn't get much over the phone interview." Sawmill moved to his desk.

"You said you spoke to them recently. What about that interview?" Wyatt asked, unable and unwilling to sit back and do nothing now that Aubrey was safely tucked away at the Butler ranch and Dade himself watched over her to ensure her safety. It might be overkill using Dade and the Butlers for that job alone but Wyatt wouldn't take chances with his little girl.

"Good point. I'll review the transcript and see if there are any clues as to where he might be taking her," Sawmill admitted as his fingers pounded the keyboard. It was better than the hen-peck method.

Wyatt moved behind the sheriff. "What are the chances he'd cross state lines?"

"It's a possibility we can't ignore, which is why I issued the BOLO."

All Wyatt cared about was bringing Meg home where she belonged. Her life might be here in Cattle Barge, but he was starting to see the possibility that his might be, too.

Whether they were in Austin or here, as long as they were together with their daughter the rest could sort itself out. She could work, not work. Hell, he didn't care one way or another as long as he got to come home to her and the baby every night.

If Wyatt strained, he could see the interview, especially after the sheriff blew up the type and leaned toward the monitor. He must have blown the document up by 140 percent.

He rubbed tired eyes and rolled his neck before straining to read the words.

Wyatt could easily see the interview from his vantage point. Since it was better to ask forgiveness than permission, he scanned the document, searching for a clue to where Jonathon might've taken Meg. All the air squeezed from his lungs thinking about harm coming to her.

The sheriff's personal cell belted out its ringtone.

"Excuse me," Sawmill said. He answered the call and immediately walked toward the hallway.

Wyatt read the entry where Jonathon had taken Mary Jane for her tenth and last birthday. To a property on the lake where the two rode horses, her favorite activity.

The only thing Wyatt was certain of was that the sheriff was on the wrong track. Send in Sawmill or one of his deputies and Jonathon might kill her.

Which left him no choice but to strike out on his own.

Chapter Fifteen

The night was pitch-black and chilly. It was the kind of dark that made it so black outside that the moon wasn't even visible.

Normally Wyatt would see this as a good opportunity to go fishing.

Now he saw it as good cover for hunting—hunting a criminal.

He cut off his truck's engine less than a mile from the site he believed Jonathon had Meg. He'd used his smartphone's GPS to find the place.

The sheriff's deputy was on the other side of the county at an abandoned strip center based on a tip from the Fjords.

On the off chance the deputy hit the nail on the head, that base was covered. Call it gut instinct or intuition, but Wyatt feared the information was wrong. He decided to take another approach in hopes one of them would find her in time.

Any other possibility had to be pushed outside the boundary of possibility.

Besides, if Jonathon and Mary Jane were as close as Meg had said, it made sense he would take Meg to the last place he remembered spending time with his sister.

According to Mrs. Fjord, the lake was Jonathon's favorite place. The property around the lake—including the stable—had since been split up to sell as lakefront property and this particular spot had been bought by a family for personal use.

When Wyatt had pulled up GPS coordinates of the area, he'd immediately locked onto the perfect building to take a hostage.

Wyatt hoped a family wasn't there or he could potentially be counting a lot of bodies. No, he stopped himself right there. This wouldn't end in tragedy. Anger fired through him, heating his skin against the frigid night air blasting toward him.

Meg had to be all right. There was no other choice.

Getting to the location without using some kind of light was impossible. So Wyatt covered his cell inside his jacket and dimmed the screen as low as it could go without losing all contrast.

Problems were mounting. What if she wasn't there? What if she was? How could he get inside the structure without alerting anyone? He'd seen a demo of shipping container homes once before, and opening the door had made more noise than an oncoming freight train. Not to mention the fact that it brought in unexpected light. He circled the building. This one had a door, at least.

But, there was no way to get any intel without breaching the building. The place was closed up tight, save for the metal door. Wyatt's biggest fear was that he wouldn't be able to see what was going on without alerting Jonathon to the fact that he was there.

Basically, he might be better off if he drove his truck straight into one wall and hoped for the best. Frustration nipped at him. There was too much on the line.

One mistake could cost him the woman he loved.

Taking her to the lake would be a stroke of genius on Jonathon's part. The sheriff had sent a deputy to the strip center and another to the site Mary Jane had last been spotted. No one would think about this place.

Wyatt fired off a text to the sheriff, letting him know that Wyatt was planning to investigate.

Stepping lightly, Wyatt followed the waterline around the lake. At least the ground was cold and hard. Sounds of night, crickets chirping and other insects filled the air. At least on the water's edge there weren't a lot of trees.

A sticky blanket of something pulled at Wyatt's face. A spiderweb?

He didn't want to think about the size of a spider it would take to make one large enough to spread from one tree to the next in this part of the terrain.

At least the cold would ward off snakes. They didn't bother him much. He just didn't need the distraction.

There were other creatures that could get the best of him in these lands. A wild boar caught off guard would be enough to do him in.

Texting the sheriff to ask for backup was the right call but waiting could cost Meg's life. If Wyatt was right and Jonathon somehow got the jump on him, Meg could pay the ultimate price anyway. Trying to do this without alerting anyone to his plans would be stupid.

What about his newfound family? Both Dade and Dalton looked like they could handle themselves in any situation. They were clearly less experienced than the sheriff and deputies but they'd seen and done more than most civilians. Wyatt didn't want to put them in jeopardy without them knowing full well what they would be signing up for.

He'd give full disclosure of the dangers.

They'd offered help before and he'd already trusted them with the care of his daughter.

Without them, he could end up dead, with no parent for Aubrey.

After evaluating his options, he determined that notifying his brothers of his location would be a smart move. Given more time, he could've come up with a better plan of attack.

Time was the enemy and he had no idea if Meg was still breathing.

Again, he wouldn't allow himself to consider the possibility that she wasn't.

He fired off a text, giving his location and brief details about his mission.

Then he put his phone on silent. If he had to sacrifice himself to ensure Aubrey grew up with a mother, he wouldn't hesitate. His own mother had been the rock in his life and most likely the reason he was a successful business-man and hadn't ended up on the wrong side of the law. The line had been blurred a few times during his rebellious teenage years, but he'd come full circle.

He'd made her proud before she died. He'd seen that in her eyes, too. Every child deserved that chance.

Wyatt moved stealthily along the shoreline as though stalking prey, the fight building inside him with every forward step. He'd tucked his Glock inside the band of his jeans and pulled his shirttail out to cover it. He'd learned a long time ago not to show his hand before he had to, and concealing his gun could keep Jonathon off balance should things go south.

He chanced a glance at his phone, check-ing his location on the map against the target. Having cell coverage here was surprising and fortunate.

The place was dead ahead. Wyatt blacked out the screen and returned his cell to his pocket. Since he'd been walking for more than twenty minutes, his eyes were adjusting to the dark.

Another advantage. He'd take what he could get and be grateful at this point.

All the windows were sealed off. Wyatt walked the perimeter trying to get a good feel for the place and what the floor plan might be.

Light spilled underneath the crack of the back door. As he made his way toward the door, it swung open. Wyatt froze.

A male stalked outside and emptied a bucket. Surely, Jonathon wouldn't be so haphazard as to leave the back door unlocked. Had Wyatt made the wrong call in coming here?

Heart hammering, he started to plan his retreat. He'd made a mistake.

The guy went back inside and closed the door. He didn't lock it, confirming what Wyatt already knew. This couldn't be the right place.

Another thought struck. Was Jonathon too confident no one would find him there?

And then he heard it. The sound, *that* sound. The heartbreaking sound of Meg crying out in pain.

Wyatt doubled back and stood at the door, listening. One noise and he'd be found out. It took all the strength he had not to throw open that door, burst into the room and take Jonathon down with his bare hands. Hell, Wyatt would shoot the man if it meant saving Meg.

Again, tipping his hand could be fatal. So he waited for Meg to scream again, clenching his back teeth so hard he thought they might crack. He fisted his free hand and released, repeating a couple of times to work off some of his tension.

And he waited.

Meg screamed again and Wyatt used the noise to cover any sounds that might come from opening the door. He cracked it enough to see Meg curled in a ball on the floor with Jonathon standing over her. Torturing her?

His gaze flew to Jonathon's hands to check for a weapon. He didn't see one, but that didn't mean one wasn't within reach.

Jonathon sounded agitated as he yelled for her to be still. He was kneeling over her, doing something with that bucket Wyatt couldn't make out.

The room was small. It wouldn't take but a couple of strides for Wyatt to bridge the distance.

Every single muscle in Wyatt's body corded as he slipped inside the door. And then Meg released a scream that nearly cracked his chest in half.

Wyatt took two giant steps before diving on top of Fjord, knocking him off balance and off Meg. Somewhere in the back of his mind it registered that Meg's hands were bound. Duct tape was over her mouth, and he had to assume that her legs were taped, as well.

Wyatt and Fjord crashed hard onto the concrete. Jonathon was small in comparison to Wyatt, but he was scrappy enough to twist onto his back and launch a knee into Wyatt's groin.

Air whooshed out of Wyatt's lungs as he tried to recover while taking an elbow to the left eye.

Meg was somewhere in the background, trying to wriggle free.

Wyatt climbed on top of Jonathon and captured him in between his powerful thigh muscles.

A fist came up so fast that it barely registered Jonathon was holding something in his hand until the object slammed into his forehead.

Momentarily stunned, Wyatt shook his head.

In the next second, he was being tossed onto his shoulder. The smaller man took full advantage of the blow that Wyatt was recovering from.

"Get out of here," Wyatt said to Meg. Out of the corner of his eye, he saw her scooting toward them. Wrong direction, he thought as something—blood?—oozed over his eye.

Jonathon was pounding Wyatt with fists, kicks. The guy was coming at Wyatt with everything he had.

Wyatt fought back, but a bout of dizziness was making it difficult to keep his bearings.

And then Meg must've done something to get Jonathon's attention because he spun around facing away from Wyatt.

That's all the leverage Wyatt needed. He forced himself to focus and then threw his arms around Jonathon's midsection, clamping his arms at his sides.

Jonathon might've caught Wyatt off guard before, but he wouldn't again.

Wyatt threw his considerable heft into Jonathon, causing him to take a couple of steps forward. This time when he fell Wyatt made sure to secure the squirrely guy beneath him, pinning his torso and arms with his thighs. Jonathon bucked, but he was no match for Wyatt's size.

And then a thought flashed in his mind. From this vantage point, Wyatt could pull out his gun and destroy Jonathon with one flick of his trigger finger.

Being a father must be softening him because he didn't want to explain himself in court or have a news story his daughter could read some day about how her father had killed a man, even this man.

Instead, Wyatt drew back his fist and punched Jonathon so hard his jaw snapped and he lost consciousness.

"Can you scoot closer to me?" he asked Meg, not daring to give an inch in case Jonathon came to and started swinging his fists again. He wouldn't underestimate the man twice.

She mumbled something that sounded like agreement, and he could see her making her way toward him.

When she was close enough, he tugged at the tape covering her mouth until it was free.

"Wyatt," she said on a gasp. "You found me."

"I will always find you."

After untying her and instructing her to call 911, Wyatt looked down at Jonathon. Tragedy had struck his family at such a young age and

Wyatt could almost sympathize. Losing his sister at such an early age had broken the man.

"Why did he want to hurt you?" Wyatt asked Meg, wrapping his arm around her.

"He said I didn't deserve a family. He ran into me in the store after Aubrey was born and something snapped. He said he never stopped blaming me for Mary Jane's death but it wasn't until he saw me with my daughter, looking happy for the first time, that he truly broke," she said with a sob.

"What about Stephanie?" he asked.

"He hated everyone connected to me. If you'd been in the picture before he would've tried to hurt you," she explained. "He said he wanted to take away everyone close to me before he ended my life."

That's where Wyatt's empathy for the man stopped. Because everyone was dealt a bad hand at some point in his or her life. Emotions like revenge or resentment made the situation so much worse, poisoning any good left in a person.

The true measure of a man wasn't what he did when he fell down. It was how he got back up and what he made of his life after.

And that made him rethink the resentments

he'd formed toward his family. And, besides, the holiday was near. Christmas was a time for miracles…

Chapter Sixteen

Meg could scarcely believe that she was still alive and that Wyatt was standing in front of her. Both of them were completely intact if not a little worse for wear. The EMT had cleared her after treating her injuries and the Butler twins had arrived with reassurances that Aubrey was safe at the ranch. Meg was pleased that her daughter's new family seemed protective of her already.

Meg's left jaw burned from the pain of several blows. Feeling was returning to her hands and Wyatt's coat was the only warmth. She wanted to hold her daughter again so badly her arms ached.

Wyatt was about the most beautiful thing she could ever see aside from Aubrey.

"I don't care where we live or why," he started, taking her hands in his. "All I know is that I want to make everything right for you, our daughter and our family."

And then he looked at her with so much love in his eyes she had to steady herself.

"I have an important question to ask, Meg Anderson." He bent down on one knee, causing what felt like a flock of birds to take flight inside her rib cage.

"I knew I was in trouble the minute we met a year ago. I was an idiot to let you walk out of my life then. But I like to think I'm smarter than that now. That I don't make the same mistakes twice. I love you. It's always been you and it always will be you." He paused like he'd already said too much and there was a moment of uncertainty in his eyes as he searched hers.

"I will never love another man as much as I love you," she said. There was so much relief playing out in his features as she said those words.

"Then there's only one thing left to ask." Another flash of uncertainty danced across his steel eyes, which disappeared the second Meg smiled. "Will you do me the incredible honor of becoming my wife?"

"I want to say yes," she hedged.

"But?"

"How will we know it's real? I mean, my hormones are out of whack and you just found out that you're a father. It's only natural to want—"

Wyatt pressed his lips to hers to stop her from finishing the sentence and she melted against him. He thoroughly kissed her, and when she was out of breath, he pulled back and looked into her eyes.

"Does that feel fake in any way to you?" he asked.

A grin tugged at the corner of her mouth so he kissed her there, too.

"Not in the least," she admitted, allowing the smile to spread. "When did you know?"

"The first time we kissed the other day. Didn't take a half second to realize in my heart that you were the only one I wanted to spend the rest of my life with. My brain took a little while to get the message, but in here—" he touched her hand to the center of his chest "—there's never been a question. At least not for me."

He released her hand and folded his arms across his chest. "But now it's your move."

The minute she smiled, he had his answer. Hearing the words was even better.

"Yes, Wyatt. I'll be your wife. I love you. It's always been you. I knew last year that I was in trouble, and I couldn't be happier to make the three of us official."

With that, he stood and took her in his arms. He said in almost a whisper against her hair, "I want to spend the rest of my life making every one of your dreams come true."

"Welcome to the family, Meg," Dalton said. It would be strange to have so many uncles, aunts and cousins for Aubrey. Meg's heart danced because she'd be gaining a family, too.

Meg had never seen Wyatt look so happy.

"I was an only child my entire life. I might not be good at being a brother, but I sure as hell promise to do my best," Wyatt said to his brothers.

Dade smiled, embraced Wyatt in a bear hug and offered his well wishes. "Ella said your daughter is the sweetest thing she's ever seen. She's sleeping like an angel and the two of you should take your time coming back." He smiled conspiratorially. "Between you and me I wouldn't be surprised if Ella made her own announcement about a baby any day now."

Dalton seemed shocked. "You think our sister's pregnant?"

"Maybe not now. But she will be. I saw the glittery look in her eyes when she first held her niece and the way she looked at her husband after."

"Holden's a good guy. He'll make a fine father someday," Dalton said.

Niece. Brothers. Family.

Wyatt completed the picture of everything Meg had ever hoped for. For *her* future and her little girl's. She couldn't wait to start their journey as a real family. There was no better time to start than Christmas.

ED STAPLES TOOK his place at the dining table at last. It had been three days since Jonathon's arrest. A wedding date had been set for the morning of New Year's Eve.

"On behalf of Mike Butler, I've been instructed to officially welcome you to the family," Ed said to Wyatt with a glance toward Meg and the baby cooing in her arms.

Wyatt thanked him as Meg smiled before returning her gaze to their daughter.

"As you all know the sheriff hasn't made any progress on your father's case. However, I've been instructed to read this letter to you. So, if everyone's ready." Ed scanned the faces at the table, looking for confirmation.

"Ed's been giving us these letters after Dad's murder, which almost makes me believe that he knew what was coming," Ella said.

"On the outside, your father seemed haphazard with the way he lived life, made his decisions," Ed said after contemplating her words for a minute.

"But I knew him better than that," Ella said.

"Maybe we'll all know at some point but he never said anything to me. His instructions were clear. If anything happened to him, read the letters he left for me in order," Ed supplied.

"Have you thought about giving them to the sheriff?" Ella asked.

"Your father was clear and he had me build in the controls to keep them out of court. If the sheriff asks, I'm to refuse. It would take a court order, but then I have controls in place to cover that base, too. Your father was always one step ahead," Ed admitted.

"Which leads me to believe that he didn't know who killed him," Ella said. "If he'd known anything was going to happen to him, he had to know there'd be chaos after his death that could put all of us in jeopardy."

"I'll reserve judgment until I open the last letter," Ed stated.

Ella gasped. She had to be thinking what Meg was... Would more Butler children come out of the woodwork?

To her credit, she'd been welcoming to Wyatt and to Meg. It was clear that she was enamored with Aubrey, and Meg suspected that Dalton had been right about what he said before. Ella would be making an announcement of her own before long. She and Holden seemed enraptured with each other, and there was a longing in Ella's eyes when she looked at the baby.

"Two letters are left. And then there's the reading of the will in a couple of days," Ed said.

"I'm guessing you haven't opened that, either," Ella said.

Ed confirmed with a nod. "I'm to open it in the presence of all Mike's children on Christmas Eve."

Conversation stilled.

Dalton finally chimed in. "It'll be strange this year."

Dade was nodding his head in agreement along with their older sister. "Did Cadence say when she was coming home?"

"Christmas Eve. She said she'll be here for the reading," Ella said.

"She's been gone too long." Dade put his hand on the table, palms down.

"We're each dealing with our father's death in our own way," Ella reminded.

Both of the twins nodded. Strange that Meg could already tell them apart. At first glance, they looked so similar it had been impossible. But as soon as she had spent a little time around them she saw the different personalities come through.

"What's in my letter?" Wyatt, who had been quiet until now, asked.

With a half smile and a nod, Ed opened the sealed envelope sitting in front of him.

Wyatt,
I won't make excuses. Your mother did right by you. I didn't. There's no reason in the world I should've allowed that to happen. I've failed as a man, as a father. But—and if you're reading this, some-thing's happened—there is something I did get right in this world. My six children. It is my sincere wish that the children who grew up under my roof haven't adopted

my cruelty. I've seen four of them band together because of me. I'm not proud of that, but I am of them. They showed me what it was like to have a family. I'm gone before I had a chance to express that I knew what that truly meant. Seeing them together, the way they supported each other. That's my real legacy. Watching it has been my greatest gift. One I didn't deserve. I hope they can embrace you and Madelyn the same. You deserve that much from me. The lake house you've been wanting is yours if you'll take it. I'd always intended to give it to your mother. She wouldn't accept it or anything else from me. She said the only hope you had of making something of yourself was to grow up like I did, with nothing. I hope you'll consider being part of this family. If not for you, then for your children. Because I can tell you from experience, walking alone in life eventually leaves you lonely.

Yours,

M.M.

Meg looked to Wyatt, whose head was bowed. She could see a tear leak from his eye as his siblings, one by one, came over to shake his hand or embrace him.

"How'd he know that I was trying to buy the lake house?" Wyatt finally asked.

Dade shrugged his shoulders and looked to Madelyn.

"He kept tabs on us over the years," she supplied. "Can't say that I'm surprised."

Meg knew for certain that the family he'd always craved was right there. For him. For Aubrey. For the three of them.

Her heart swelled as they hugged her and took turns marveling at their little girl, touching her cheek or her tiny hand. Aubrey welcomed all the attention.

"Welcome to Hereford ranch officially," Dalton finally said. "This is as much your place as it is ours. Every family member has a home and a job here. And we're looking forward to starting new Christmas traditions with our expanding family."

Dade added, "We can be overwhelming at times but you'll never find more caring than with this crazy bunch. Welcome to the family."

"Glad to finally be home," Wyatt said.

Dalton shook Wyatt's hand before saying, "I'm proud to be your brother. Now let's fire up the barbecue grill and celebrate Texas style so we can plan a proper Christmas together."

Wyatt shot a smile at Meg, a real smile. And she could see that they finally fit in somewhere. Together. As a family. With a real place to call home.

* * * * *

Look for the next book in USA Today *bestselling author Barb Han's Crisis: Cattle Barge miniseries,* Murder And Mistletoe, *available next month.*

And don't miss the previous books in the series:
Sudden Setup
Endangered Heiress
Texas Grit

Available now from Harlequin Intrigue!

Get 4 FREE REWARDS!

We'll send you 2 FREE Books plus 2 FREE Mystery Gifts.

Harlequin® Romantic Suspense books feature heart-racing sensuality and the promise of a sweeping romance set against the backdrop of suspense.

FREE
Value Over
$20

YES! Please send me 2 FREE Harlequin® Romantic Suspense novels and my 2 FREE gifts (gifts are worth about $10 retail). After receiving them, if I don't wish to receive any more books, I can return the shipping statement marked "cancel." If I don't cancel, I will receive 4 brand-new novels every month and be billed just $4.99 per book in the U.S. or $5.74 per book in Canada. That's a savings of at least 12% off the cover price! It's quite a bargain! Shipping and handling is just 50¢ per book in the U.S. and 75¢ per book in Canada*. I understand that accepting the 2 free books and gifts places me under no obligation to buy anything. I can always return a shipment and cancel at any time. The free books and gifts are mine to keep no matter what I decide.

240/340 HDN GMYZ

Name (please print)

Address   Apt. #

City   State/Province   Zip/Postal Code

Mail to the **Reader Service:**
IN U.S.A.: P.O. Box 1341, Buffalo, NY 14240-8531
IN CANADA: P.O. Box 603, Fort Erie, Ontario L2A 5X3

Want to try two free books from another series? Call 1-800-873-8635 or visit www.ReaderService.com.

---

*Terms and prices subject to change without notice. Prices do not include applicable taxes. Sales tax applicable in N.Y. Canadian residents will be charged applicable taxes. Offer not valid in Quebec. This offer is limited to one order per household. Books received may not be as shown. Not valid for current subscribers to Harlequin® Romantic Suspense books. All orders subject to approval. Credit or debit balances in a customer's account(s) may be offset by any other outstanding balance owed by or to the customer. Please allow 4 to 6 weeks for delivery. Offer available while quantities last.

Your Privacy—The Reader Service is committed to protecting your privacy. Our Privacy Policy is available online at www.ReaderService.com or upon request from the Reader Service. We make a portion of our mailing list available to reputable third parties that offer products we believe may interest you. If you prefer that we not exchange your name with third parties, or if you wish to clarify or modify your communication preferences, please visit us at www.ReaderService.com/consumerschoice or write to us at Reader Service Preference Service, P.O. Box 9062, Buffalo, NY 14240-9062. Include your complete name and address.

HRS18